D1168694

WITHDRAWN

Bessica Lefter Bites Back

Bessica Lefter
bites back

KRISTEN TRACY

Delacorte Press

Text copyright © 2012 by Kristen Tracy
Jacket photograph copyright © 2012 by Dean Turpin

All rights reserved. Published in the United States by Delacorte Press, an imprint of Random House Children's Books, a division of Random House, Inc., New York.

Delacorte Press is a registered trademark and the colophon is a trademark of Random House, Inc.

randomhouse.com/kids

Educators and librarians, for a variety of teaching tools, visit us at randomhouse.com/teachers

Library of Congress Cataloging-in-Publication Data is available upon request.
ISBN 978-0-385-74069-2 (hc) — ISBN 978-0-375-98961-2 (lib. bdg.) —
ISBN 978-0-375-89983-6 (ebook)

The text of this book is set in 12.5-point Apollo MT.
Book design by Heather Daugherty

Printed in the United States of America

APR 1 0 2012   10 9 8 7 6 5 4 3 2 1

First Edition

Random House Children's Books supports the First Amendment
and celebrates the right to read.

For Ulla Frederiksen and Fred Bueltmann.
You make my life bigger and better
and horse populated.

ACKNOWLEDGMENTS

Writing acknowledgments always reminds me that I'm a lucky, lucky girl. Because I get to reflect on all the people in my life who offer me unending encouragement in the form of baked goods, long walks, and motivational text messages. Many thanks to Joen Madonna, Stacey Kade, Dana Reinhardt, Tracy Roberts, Nina LaCour, Brandi Dougherty, Robin Wasserman, Julie Romeis, Christopher Benz, Sara Michas Martin, Maria Finn, Jennifer Laughran, Amy Stewart, Cory Grimminck, Regina Marler, Lea Beresford, Ayelet Waldman, Emily Schultz, and Brian Evenson. And thanks to all the gardeners on Alcatraz who keep me grounded; I'm looking at you, Shelagh Fritz, Dick Miner, Karolina Park, Monica Beary, and Marnie Beard. Extra-special thanks to Wyatt Richards for introducing me to the world of Roosevelt Middle School. Extra-extra-special thanks to Kristin Scheel for sharing her Wyatt, and providing such a story-filled friendship. Double thanks to my family, especially my dad, who took me on an inspiring trip to Bear World that I will never, ever forget. Triple thanks to Wendy Loggia, my brilliant editor, who helps make my books as funny and real as possible. Quadruple thanks to Heather Daugherty for creating a fantastic book cover that I want to both bite and frame. And quintuple thanks to Sara Crowe, my agent and friend. You make everything better.

THINGS TO AVOID IN MIDDLE SCHOOL

1. Homework
2. Jerks
3. Cruddy bear paws
4. Wars of texts
5. Possibly Raya Papas

CHAPTER

I had forgotten something important, and no matter how hard I tried to make myself remember it, I couldn't. My mother and I were on the way to my best friend Sylvie's house. Sylvie and I were going to plan her upcoming birthday party minute by minute. It needed to be crammed full of games and cake and craziness. You only turned twelve once. I tapped my temple, trying to remember the thing I'd forgotten. *Tap. Tap. Tap.* Out the window, I caught glimpses of my neighborhood as it whooshed by. A house. A lawn. A house. A lawn. Hay fields. Cows. My gorgeous neighbor, Noll Beck, atop a trotting horse.

"Ooh," I said, sticking my finger on the window, pointing to Noll and the trotter. But then they were gone.

"What?" my mother asked. She patted my knee. "Are you afraid Sylvie's mom might snap at you because she's under a tight doll-assembly deadline?"

I looked at my mother in surprise. "I didn't know anything about a tight doll-assembly deadline." Sylvie's mom painted the eyelashes on ceramic doll heads. And even though I didn't understand how this could be true, it appeared that demand for these dolls and their black spidery lashes kept growing and growing and growing.

My mother pulled into Sylvie's driveway. "Mrs. Potaski mentioned it to me on the phone. She sounded stressed-out."

"This is terrible," I said. I'd barely made up with Sylvie and won back the right to see her. I didn't want her mom to snap at me.

"It's not terrible, Bessica. Just be on your best behavior."

"I can do that." I reached for the door handle.

"And don't forget to ask Sylvie what she wants for her birthday," my mom said. "The scoping phase is over. We need to track down her gift and get it."

My mom made buying Sylvie's birthday present sound like hunting for a moose. It bummed me out to hear that the scoping phase was over. Because that was my favorite phase. I sighed.

"Actually, Mom, that's not the plan," I said. Then I stopped opening my door, because it was pretty clear to me that I was going to have to explain the plan to my mom.

"What plan?" my mom asked.

I sighed again. And when I did this I noticed that my breath smelled like breakfast sausage. "I want Sylvie's present to be a total surprise. So today I'm going to trick her into telling me the top three things that she wants." I smiled slyly when I said this, because I was pretty proud of my plan. Then I reached in my pocket and pulled out a piece of gum and chomped on it.

"Why don't you just ask her what she wants?" my mother said. "Be straightforward about it."

I let out a big peppermint-sausage breath of disapproval. "Mom, birthdays are about surprising people you care about with what they most want in the world. If you don't surprise them, then you haven't done it right. It's a basic birthday rule."

It alarmed me to think that my mom didn't know basic birthday rules. I opened the door and got out of the car.

"If you need me I'll be down the street," my mom said.

But I already knew this. Because it was the fourth time my mother had told me that she would be down the street.

"I might walk over when I'm finished," I said. Alma, the new office assistant where my mom worked, had invited her to play croquet. And though I'd only played croquet once, I remembered really enjoying swinging my mallet.

My mother frowned. "Call before you come. And walk through the field to get there. Not the road."

I nodded. My mom started to back out of the driveway, but then she stopped, lowered her window, and hollered to me.

I ran to her door. I was hoping maybe she wanted to give me emergency money. Sometimes she did that after she dropped me off.

"Yes?" I said, holding out my hand.

"Bessica, sometimes women put too much pressure on themselves to make everything perfect. I don't want to see you burden yourself that way."

I kept holding my hand out, waiting for money. But she didn't give me any. She just kept talking.

"You don't need to trick Sylvie into telling you what she wants for her birthday. Do the easy thing and just ask her." My mom smiled at me in a huge way. Then she slapped my hand and cheered, "Right on!"

Things felt very weird in Sylvie's driveway. I kept my hand lifted and my mom slapped it again. "Seize the day!" *Seize the day?* In all my life my mother had never said anything that lame to me before in a driveway. My mouth fell open a little bit in disgust, and my gum toppled out and landed in the grass.

"You lost your gum," my mom said.

"I know. I'm trying to understand *why* you're saying *what* you're saying."

My mom's smile grew bigger. "I'm glad we had this talk too. It's a relief."

"A relief?" I said. Why did saying lame things to me in Sylvie Potaski's driveway make my mother feel relieved?

"And I want you to know that this is how we're going to talk to each other from now on, like adults. I'm not going to treat you like a child anymore."

This was pretty terrible news. Why would I want my mom to talk to me like I was an adult? That was how she talked to my dad, and Grandma Lefter, and Grandma's terrible boyfriend, Willy, and bank tellers, and all the patients getting toe surgeries at the podiatrist's office, and a bunch of other people, like our mail carrier. Bleh.

"Mom," I said. "That's weird. And I'm going to follow my birthday rules and trick Sylvie into telling me what she wants, because that's the whole point of having a birthday. Getting surprised by the perfect gift." I looked my mom right in the eye when I said that, because my birthday was in four months, and I was hoping for a surprise party with a bunch of perfect, surprising gifts. And I did not want perfect, surprising *adult* gifts.

My mother sighed and looked disappointed. "Try to have a good time."

"Okay," I chirped. Then I turned around and ran as fast as I could toward Sylvie's front door.

I rang the doorbell like a very polite person. And I waited for Sylvie's mom to answer. Sylvie's mom did scare me a little bit. Because even when she wasn't stressed-out, we didn't always get along. When she banned me from seeing Sylvie, it was because she'd gotten it into her head that I was a bad influence on her daughter. And in addition to enforcing that ban, she also switched Sylvie to a different school. And that had been about a month ago. So things were still a little tense.

"Bessica!" Mrs. Potaski said. She smiled when she saw me, and this made my stomach feel dance-happy and wonderful.

"I brought you something," I said. I set my backpack on the floor and opened it. Then I carefully pulled out a sack with a blueberry tart in it. "It's a tart."

Mrs. Potaski stopped smiling. "Bessica, thank you for the tart. But you shouldn't feel like you need to bring me a tart every time you come over."

But that was exactly how I felt. Because I worried that at any moment, Sylvie's mom might stop liking me and ban me again.

"Bessica!" Sylvie yelled. I saw her at the top of her hall-way. Then she ran full speed toward me and did some excited jumping. I hoped her mom noticed all the jumping. Because it was pretty clear to me that Sylvie should switch middle schools and come to mine. Sixth grade would be a lot better if she did that.

"Let's go to my room and plan the party!" she said.

"Okay!" I said. And then I forgot all about being a polite person and I ran through the Potaskis' house with my shoes on, yelling, "Party time!"

Sylvie shut her bedroom door. "I'm going with a disco theme!"

I plopped onto the floor and didn't get excited at all when she said this, because over the summer she'd told me she was going to go with a jungle theme, so all the ideas I had were jungle-based.

"What's wrong?" Sylvie asked, plopping on the floor next to me.

"What happened to our great jungle idea?" I asked.
Sylvie shrugged.

"Maybe we should brainstorm," I said. We had to do that in public speaking all the time. We wasted a ton of paper doing it, but I always ended up with at least one good topical idea.

"But I already designed invitations," Sylvie told me. She turned on her computer and showed me the ecard with pink roller skates.

"Cool," I said. Then I tapped my temple. *Tap. Tap. Tap.*

"Why are you touching your head?" Sylvie asked.

I frowned. "I think I forgot something."

Sylvie shrugged. "Let's plan my disco party and maybe it will come to you."

"Okay," I said.

So I started thinking about Sylvie's party, and my mind took off like a rocket. But I couldn't make it stay focused on disco stuff. It kept brainstorming jungle ideas. "You're going to need a ton of cool crud," I said. "Coconuts. Palm trees. A tiger piñata. Grass skirts. Fake parrots. An inflatable volcano."

"That's not disco," Sylvie said. "That's jungle."

"Yeah," I said. And we both just looked at each other. "Maybe you could have a double theme?"

"Maybe," she said.

It was thrilling to hear her be so positive.

"If we get our butts in gear, I bet we have time to make at least four piñatas!" Last year, when we read *A Wrinkle in Time,* Sylvie and I had made an IT piñata for extra credit. It had turned out pretty cool. Except for the caved-in brain area.

"Whoa," Sylvie said. "Four piñatas? That's extravagant."

My eyes got very big when she said this. "Exactly. You will have the most extravagant disco/jungle party ever!"

Sylvie looked doubtful. But I kept making the list. "We'll also need torches and stuffed monkeys. And maybe some safari hats."

"I'll ask my mom to buy butcher paper and we can draw a lot of this stuff," Sylvie said.

I folded my arms across my chest in a disapproving way. I didn't know how she planned to draw an inflatable volcano or a safari hat.

"I'm not a millionaire," Sylvie said.

And when she said that I felt bad for both of us. Because if Sylvie had been a millionaire, we'd have been able to plan a much better disco/jungle party.

"Let's focus on my guest list," Sylvie said.

"Okay."

We scooted closer together. I really liked hanging out with Sylvie. Lately, Sylvie liked hanging out with her new friend Malory and Malory's ferret. And while I didn't hate Malory, I also didn't enjoy spending time with her or the ferret. Sylvie was my best friend. We didn't need anybody else in the picture.

"What about Angel Karlinsky?" Sylvie asked.

I had never met this person. Sylvie went to South Teton Middle School and had a ton of friends, and I went to North Teton Middle School and had basically zero friends; we ran in different crowds now.

"How many people do you get to invite, again?" I asked.

Sylvie sighed like she was sick of answering that question. "Fourteen."

"That's right," I said. I kept forgetting that number

because it didn't make any sense to me. Ten made sense because that was a common unit of people measurement. And twelve made sense because that was a common unit of donut measurement. But fourteen? I'd never heard of that being a unit of measurement for anything.

Then I got a great idea and I squealed, "I know exactly who you should invite to your party!"

"Really?" Sylvie asked. She sounded very skeptical. Maybe because we didn't know the same people.

I tapped the invitation on the screen. "Invite the richest kids at your school, because they'll give you the best presents."

Sylvie frowned. "That's a terrible idea, Bessica."

I frowned back at her. It didn't feel pleasant to have my idea judged so harshly like that by my best friend.

"I want to invite somebody from each of my classes. That's six. And you and Malory. That's eight. And then there are four girls I really like in my dance class—Dinesh, Winnie, Iris, and Kirby."

"You know a person named Dinesh?" I asked. Because that seemed like a weird name for a girl or a boy.

Sylvie nodded. "So that's twelve. And then I was thinking I'd let you invite somebody."

"Really?" I asked. That was so sweet of Sylvie. I considered the possibilities. Then I felt panicked and my breathing got breathy, because I didn't know if I knew anybody at my school well enough to invite them to Sylvie's party. I'd started middle school with a brand-new haircut and no friends. I'd been eating lunch with Annabelle Deeter and her friends for a while now, but I hadn't seen any of them in their bare feet. And I hadn't been invited to their houses. Also, I'd never seen their baby albums. So we weren't that close yet. I watched Sylvie type Kirby's email address.

"I can't decide who to invite," I said. "Can I tell you later?"

Sylvie didn't look thrilled.

"Please?" I asked. Sylvie had never turned me down before when I used that word. The trick was to say it in a way that sounded very sincere.

"I don't want to put you in a tough position. Is one invitation not enough?" Sylvie asked.

"Oh, it's definitely enough." One invitation was plenty. I just needed to make the best choice possible.

"You could always ask Alice Potgeiser," Sylvie said. "That would be a good way to get to know the other half mascot."

My mind zoomed so fast it almost knocked me down. I finally remembered what I had forgotten.

"What's wrong?" Sylvie asked. "You looked really freaked out."

I couldn't speak.

"Do you need some water?" Sylvie asked.

I shook my head. "I'm not supposed to be here," I said. The words tumbled out of me.

"Why not?" Sylvie asked. She stared at me with a bunch of concern on her face.

"I'm supposed to be at school!" I said.

Sylvie blinked at me. Sylvie was always blinking. "It's teacher in-service day. Why?"

I reached out and grabbed her hand. "Because today was the day we divided the mascot schedule." I couldn't make my mind stop zooming. Alice had hated me even before we both competed for school mascot. After everybody had voted and we ended up tying, Alice Potgeiser's hate for me quadrupled. If I wasn't there to divide the schedule, she was going to make me cheer against all the mascots she thought were cruddy. I gasped. All my efforts to build an awesome new reputation would be flushed down the toilet.

"Won't everything get split fairly?" Sylvie asked.

Sylvie was very naïve. I rolled my eyes. "You're in middle school. You know the answer." I thought back to the assembly where Alice and I had competed in front of everybody. She was so vicious-looking in her fake bear head. There was no way she'd split things fairly.

I collapsed into a lying-down position. The room spun around me.

"Bessica," Sylvie said, lowering her face to look into mine. "I think you're overreacting."

I stared up at Sylvie. I could see right up her nose. Her nostrils looked like dark caves covered in hair. I sure hoped that wasn't what my nose looked like when people stared up it. I closed my eyes very tightly.

"Don't freak out," Sylvie said.

I couldn't believe that Sylvie didn't have any sympathy for me. "I'm doomed."

Sylvie flicked me with her finger. And that surprised me. Because she'd never finger-flicked me before. Middle school was really changing her. "Just call the school and let them know there was a mix-up."

Wow. Sylvie had never come up with a solution to a problem before either. Usually that was my job. This felt a little weird. I reached for my backpack and my cell phone but my fingers were trembling too much to dial. And then I remembered something else, and it made me cry a little. "We were going to get fitted for the costume today." There was no way Alice and I were the same size. So the bear mascot outfit would get fitted to her and she'd look neat and wonderful and I'd look floppy and not very ferocious. I moaned again.

"It's not the end of the world," Sylvie said.

But that was exactly what it was. Why couldn't Sylvie see that?

Sylvie took my phone out of my hand and smiled. "Don't worry, Bessica. I'll help you."

Even though it felt weird and I was a little unsure about it, I let Sylvie Potaski use my phone and fix my life. Only that wasn't what happened. No. No. No. After I gave Sylvie my phone, things in my life didn't get any better. They got much, much, much worse.

CHAPTER

Before Sylvie could call the school, my phone buzzed.

"That might be my grandma," I told her. Ever since Grandma had run off with her Internet boyfriend to climb around in caves, she hadn't been calling me as much as she used to.

I thought Sylvie would hand over my phone, but she just kept trying to solve my problem. And she answered the call. It was very weird to watch Sylvie behave this way.

"Hello?" Sylvie said. "No, this is not Bessica Lefter."

When Sylvie used my last name, I stopped thinking that Grandma Lefter was calling me.

"Let me see if I can find her," Sylvie said.

Sylvie looked a little freaked out. She covered the receiver with her hand and whispered, "It's your principal!"

I gasped. "You shouldn't have answered it!"

"But I did!" she said.

The terribleness of my situation hit me very quickly: Sylvie Potaski was not good at solving my problems.

"Tell her I'm in the hospital," I said.

"I'm not going to lie," Sylvie said.

"Well, you can't tell her I'm sitting at your house planning your disco/jungle–theme birthday party. It'll look like I don't care about being mascot. She might strip me of my mascot duties and give them all to Alice."

"Cookies are ready!" Sylvie's mom called.

"Shhh," I said. I sure hoped Principal Tidge hadn't heard her. Because that wasn't something people hollered in hospitals.

Sylvie lifted the phone to her face. "I'm still looking for her."

"Why would you still be looking for me if I'm at the hospital?" I whispered. "That doesn't make sense. They make you stay in your room until they discharge you in a wheelchair."

Sylvie looked like she didn't know what do.

"Please don't ruin my life," I said. "Please just tell a good lie for me. Just this once."

Sylvie took a big breath. "Bessica is resting."

And then, so Sylvie wouldn't be lying as much, I flattened down on the floor like I was sleeping.

"Um, you're asking me if she's sick?" Sylvie said, looking at me.

I nodded with a lot of energy and also stuck out my tongue and moaned.

"Sort of," Sylvie said.

I bolted upright. "Not 'sort of,'" I whispered. "I *am* sick. Lie! Lie! Please. It's easy!"

I jumped to my feet, but my shoe twisted and I bent my ankle funny and I fell down.

"She's hurt," Sylvie said nervously.

Uh-oh. Sylvie shouldn't have told my principal that. I was a mascot. Injuries could get me sidelined. I shook my head no, no, no. Then I rubbed my ankle, because it did hurt a little, and then I realized my socks were itchy, so I kicked off my shoe and scratched my foot through my sock.

"She has a foot fungus. And her, um, treatment has her, uh, immobilized."

My mouth dropped open. It was like my best friend had gone crazy and decided to hate me at the same time.

"I'll give her the message," Sylvie said. Then she hung up the phone and I started yelling at her.

"What's wrong with you?" I asked.

"I can't lie!" Sylvie said.

"Of course you can. You just did! I don't have a foot fungus!" I put my shoe back on.

"Remember that one time you went barefoot in the showers at the public pool and you thought you had athlete's foot and your toes itched for a month?" Sylvie asked.

"That was in third grade!" I said. "And it turned out my cheap, imported socks were the problem."

"I know. I know. But when I saw you scratch your foot it was all I could think of," Sylvie explained.

"What if she tells Alice Potgeiser?" I asked. "I'll be so unpopular nobody will want to cheer for me."

"Okay," Sylvie said. "We can fix this."

But I didn't really believe that at this point. I didn't want Sylvie to ever try to fix anything for me again.

"Right now we have a bigger problem," Sylvie said.

This panicked me. My current problem was so enormous, I couldn't imagine a bigger one.

"Your principal is going to call your mother to reschedule your mascot fitting."

"But what if Principal Tidge brings up the fungus problem and my mother tells her that I don't have a fungus problem and that I'm at your house planning a birthday party?" I slapped my forehead. My life hadn't felt this miserable in a long, long time.

"That would be a rough night at the disco," Sylvie said.

"What?" I asked. Why was Sylvie talking about disco dancing when my life was falling apart?

"That's something Malory and I say when something goes really wrong," Sylvie said.

I pointed my finger at her face. I felt panicked and annoyed at the same time. "You're obsessed with disco!"

I took my phone back from Sylvie and tried to call my mom. But her phone went to voice mail. Which was terrible. Because it meant that my mom was either ignoring me or already talking to somebody. Maybe Principal Tidge.

Knock. Knock. Knock. Sylvie's mom opened the door and looked in at us. "Is everything okay? I can hear yelling."

Of course Mrs. Potaski could hear yelling. I didn't have time to politely explain to her *why* she heard it. I needed to get to Alma's croquet game and talk to my mom so she would know she was supposed to lie to my principal and tell her I'd been immobilized by foot fungus.

"I've got to go!" I said.

"But I'm supposed to feed you lunch," Mrs. Potaski said.

"It's okay. I'll eat something at the croquet game!" Then I sped out of Sylvie's house and headed to the back field and ran through shoulder-high weeds all the way to Alma's. When I got there, I had quite a few pieces of field grass stuck in my shoes and I was covered with cockle-burs. Plus, my legs were all scratched up.

"Mom! Mom!" I yelled as I ran over to her.

"I thought you were going to call before you came," she said, holding her mallet still.

And just then her phone started ringing. I threw my arms around her. "Don't answer that!"

"What's going on?" my mom asked. She tried to make me release my squeeze on her. But I didn't.

"Is this your daughter?" a woman asked.

We both ignored her. Because that was a dumb question.

"Mom," I said. "I have a serious, serious problem. It's vital."

"You're not making any sense, Bessica," my mom said. "Who's calling me? Is everything okay with Mrs. Potaski?"

I felt my mother reach for her phone and I snatched it out of her hands.

"Mom!" I said. "You can't talk to this person until I explain the situation to you!"

I did not want to tell everybody that my principal was calling. And I also didn't want to discuss "the situation" in front of them. For the first time I looked around at all the women at the party. They were all wearing more makeup than I thought necessary to play croquet.

"Who's calling me?" my mother asked.

She moved closer to me like she was still interested in answering her phone. So I jogged backward a little bit and leaped over a wicket.

"Mom!" I said. "Wait!" I was bummed out that my mom couldn't demonstrate more patience.

My mom's phone finally chimed that the caller had left a message.

"Bessica, let's pursue this conversation off the playing field," my mom said.

She seemed angry. She took her mallet and walked stiffly toward the part of the lawn that wasn't mowed.

"What's this about?" she asked. "And give me my phone back."

But I didn't want to give her the phone until we were both on the same page.

"Mom," I said. "Sylvie ruined my life."

"How does this involve my phone?"

I released a big breath. I didn't know where to start, so I spilled everything.

"Today was the day we divided mascot duties and got fitted for the costume," I said. "I was supposed to be at school."

"Shoot!" my mom said. Then she smacked herself on the forehead with the heel of her hand. "I totally forgot."

This made me feel better, because it was beginning to

look like my terrible situation could be blamed a little bit on my mother.

"Principal Tidge called me," I said. "And Sylvie accidentally answered my phone. And I didn't want to tell Principal Tidge I was planning a birthday party, because that would make me look like a slacker who lacked team spirit."

"Riiight . . . ," my mom said slowly.

Explaining this to my mom was turning out to be easier than I'd thought it would be.

"And then Sylvie's mom yelled that our cookies were done. And I worried that Principal Tidge would think I'd missed the meeting because I liked eating cookies more than being mascot. And then I worried she'd think I was such a gigantic slacker that I didn't even *deserve* to be mascot."

"Don't cry, Bessica. Everybody knows you're not a gigantic slacker," my mom said.

I was glad my mom said that, because I hadn't even realized I was crying.

"Things aren't as bad as they feel," she told me.

So I gave her her phone and watched her listen to the message. Her face frowned.

"Okay. I understand why you didn't want to tell Principal Tidge you were planning a party and eating cookies.

But why does she think you have an immobilizing fungus issue?"

"Sylvie told her that," I said.

"Why would Sylvie tell her that? Have your toes been itching again?"

"No!" I said. I couldn't believe my mother would ask me that at a croquet game. "Sylvie answered my phone and lost her mind." I spun my finger next to my head. "I don't know what they're teaching her at South, but she's behaving like a totally different person."

"Okay," my mom said. "All we need to do is call Principal Tidge and tell her there's been a misunderstanding."

But this made me want to cry a little bit more.

"What's wrong?" my mother asked me.

"Okay. I'm going to talk to you like we're both adults," I said, sniffling. "Middle school isn't like elementary school at all. Middle school is a heinous place that can kill you."

"Let's not take things over the top," my mom said.

I held my hand up to let her know that she should stop interrupting me. Because I was saying very serious things. "It's nothing like fifth grade. You aren't guaranteed good grades and friends and a classroom pet. You have to earn everything."

"I know it's a big transition," my mother said.

I reached out and took her hand. "Mom, the only way to survive middle school and enjoy yourself is to find your spot. When you start you don't have a spot. You have to make one by becoming something interesting like a cheerleader or hall monitor or yearbook photographer. I'm the mascot. And I don't want to lose my spot." I could feel more tears forming behind my eyes.

"Oh, Bessica," my mom said.

"And I don't want people to think I have fungus either."

My mother ran her hand through my hair. "You're not going to lose your spot. And we'll explain to Principal Tidge that your feet are fine."

"But then why did I miss the meeting today?" I whined.

I could think of a lot of great reasons why I'd missed today's meeting. But they were all lies. And I knew my mom wouldn't lie to my principal for me. Because my mom liked being honest. It was a huge bummer.

"Do you want Principal Tidge to think you've got a fungal foot infection?"

I sniffled. When she put it that way, I wasn't sure. "Becoming a mascot is the best thing that's ever happened to me, and I don't want to jeopardize it."

"Bessica," my mother said, in a tired tone. "I'll make an appointment to meet with her and we'll straighten everything out. I'm sure telling the truth won't jeopardize anything."

My mom sounded really confident. I let out a sigh, and my mother put her arm around me. "Did you figure out what Sylvie wants for her birthday?"

I had forgotten that was my job. And to be honest, when I thought about Sylvie, I got a little bit mad at her. Because until she told Principal Tidge I had foot fungus, my problem was very fixable.

"We don't have a lot of time," my mom said.

I thought about Sylvie and what she deserved. And the perfect present popped into my brain.

"Yes. I know what I want to get her," I said.

"Do we need to go to the mall after croquet?" she asked.

"Yes," I said. "The mall would be perfect."

My mom smiled. "What are you getting her?"

I smiled too. "I can't tell you. I want it to be a big surprise."

CHAPTER

Sylvie called me three times that weekend, but I never called her back. I was so mad I didn't even listen to her messages. She also texted, "So worried for you! Call me as soon as you know anything."

But I didn't plan to text her until I'd forgiven her. And I wasn't sure when that would happen.

I carefully loaded all my homework into my backpack and slid my cell phone into the front pocket. Even though we were banned from using them at school, it was nice to have it in case there was an emergency. Or in case I wanted to text Grandma Lefter at lunch because I was bored. As long as I was sneaky and nobody ever saw me using it, I knew I'd never have a problem. My backpack was so stuffed it was hard to zip it up. But I finally did. Then I dragged it down the hallway to the front door.

"I've made a surprise egg dish for breakfast," my mom said. "A frittata!"

That was not what I wanted to hear. Because in nutrition my assignment was to make a collage of all the food I ate for two weeks. And I didn't know where to find a picture of a frittata.

I sat down and stared at an egg glob with toasty brown parts on it. Sometimes surprises weren't good.

"What is this again?" I asked.

"A frittata," my mother said. "Alma gave me the recipe."

I poked at it.

"You'll like it!" she said. "It has cheese."

That did sound good, so I took a little bite. My frittata was actually very tasty.

"Wow. Your backpack looks like you stuffed a dog inside it," my mom said.

I frowned. "No, it doesn't." Then I looked at my backpack. It was pretty loaded.

"Did you finish your math worksheets?" my mom asked.

But before I could answer, I felt somebody grab me from behind. And I screamed.

"Calm down, sunshine," my dad said. "It's me."

"Okay," I said. "But it's hard for me to know that when you're standing directly behind me."

"Care for some frittata?" my mom asked.

"Indeed I would," he said.

Once a month, my dad had a morning meeting at the bread supplier warehouse, which meant he had to drive an hour and a half to Pocatello. So instead of sleeping in, he got up at the crack of dawn with the rest of us.

As soon as my mom put the frittata down in front of him, he cut it apart with his fork and started chomping on it.

"So what's in the backpack?" my dad asked. "A Shetland pony?"

My family was starting to make me feel self-conscious about the size of my school belongings.

"We were just talking about that," my mom said.

"You might need to graduate to roller luggage," my dad said. "It's better for the back."

I opened my mouth a little bit in horror.

Then my mom went over and lifted up my backpack. "Wow. It's heavy," she said. "What *have* you got inside here?"

And instead of just saying *homework,* I decided to impress her by listing everything in there.

"Clean PE clothes. A jump rope. My list of foods that

will ruin your heart for nutrition. My permanent homework for English."

And then because I wasn't sure if my parents remembered what that was, I explained it.

"Three times a week Mr. Val gives us a poem to take
home and we have to read it aloud and in our head and
write a response paragraph."

"Mr. Val plays the flute music, right?" my mom asked.

I nodded, ate more frittata, and continued explaining.

"This time, I had to respond to a fish poem by Elizabeth
Bishop."

"Neat," my dad said.

But I wanted him to be more impressed, so I explained a
bit more. "She wrote a long poem about catching a trout
and then seeing her own reflection in its eyeball. Then
the boat's gasoline made a rainbow and she tossed it back
in the water."

"I think I've read that poem," my mom said.

"Cool." But I didn't really want to get into a conversation about the fish poem with my mom. "And I have math
worksheets." But I didn't explain those because I hated
math. "And I have my map where I drew the imaginary
line of the Arctic Circle around the top of the world."

"You're still studying the Arctic?" my dad asked.

I was surprised my dad asked me this, because it was

like he'd forgotten everything I'd told him about Mr. Hoser and his iceberg ties and his deep love of blubber mitts.

"I don't think Mr. Hoser wants to study anything but the Arctic," I said.

"You can't study that for a whole year," my mom said.

"I don't know," I said. "He's contacted NASA and we have a live feed of the Arctic that we watch on Fridays."

"Wow," my dad said. "I'd like to see that."

But I was pretty sure that if my dad was forced to watch the live feed every Friday and then write a response paragraph, he wouldn't feel that way.

I cleared my throat and kept listing the contents of my backpack.

"And for public speaking I read a speech by Spock from *The Wrath of Khan,* and today we're going to watch it and analyze its structure."

My parents both looked at each other. And then at me.

"You know that Spock is a fictional character, right?" my dad asked.

"I know," I said. "He's Vulcan. Our teacher explained that already."

My parents looked at each other again. I scooped up more frittata and ate it. Then I looked at the clock.

"Hasta la vista," I said, getting up.

"Your mom isn't driving you?" my dad asked.

"Why would I be driving her?" my mom asked. "I've got to go to work and then get off early to meet with Principal Tidge."

I was a little bit nervous about this meeting.

"Why couldn't you fix things over the phone? Or email?" I asked. That seemed simpler.

"I told you. She wants all three of us to meet so we can sort through the situation," my mom said.

"Am I going to have to show her my feet?" I asked. That worried me because I hadn't trimmed my toenails for a while.

My mother wrinkled her forehead like she didn't know the answer. "Let's just wait and see what happens."

"Okay," I said. Even though I found waiting pretty painful.

"Do you want me to drive you?" my dad asked.

I didn't need that. I might not have trimmed my toenails, but I wasn't a child. I could carry a heavy backpack and get to school on a bus.

"Door-to-door service, and I might have a limited edition snack pack of Two-Taste Teton donuts in the car," he said.

"Ooh," I said. Maybe having Dad drive me was the way to go. Because the snack packs of Two-Taste Teton donuts had sold out at stores weeks ago, so I'd look very special eating them in front of everybody at lunch.

"Don't give her junk food," my mom said.

But I didn't mind that idea. Because in addition to being hard to find, Two-Taste Teton donuts were also very interesting snacks. Using technology known as flavor flecking, the company that manufactured the donuts managed to put two flavors in each donut. Plus, the wrapper had a picture of the donuts that I could use for my nutrition collage.

"Let's roll!" my dad said, getting out of his chair.

He picked up my backpack and carried it to the car. He gave me my donuts as soon as we sat down.

"These are so cool!" I said. I set my donuts on my armrest so they wouldn't get smooshed. I wanted them to look perfect when I ate them in front of everybody.

The sun hadn't risen yet. Nobody would ever send elementary school students to school in the dark. As we drove through the darkness, I listened to my dad complain about Yancey, who hadn't been documenting and disposing of his day-old bread and snack cakes properly. And I didn't really have anything to say about that.

I think my dad could tell I was bored. Because when he pulled into my school's unloading zone he said, "I'm really proud of you." He cleared his throat and sounded very serious. "I can't wait to see you perform at your first game."

I couldn't wait for that either. "Thanks," I said.

But I didn't get out of the car, because it seemed like my dad wanted to keep telling me stuff.

"Maybe we should plan a trip to Bear Galaxy soon so you can get some firsthand bear information."

"That sounds awesome!" We hadn't been to Bear Galaxy in years because it cost almost thirty dollars per vehicle to enter. It was a place where they kept bears behind fences so you could drive around and look at them all day long.

"I can remember my dad driving me to this very building when I was your age," he said.

"Uh-huh," I said. I was starting to worry that I was going to be late.

"Life goes by so fast. *Bam!* You're in middle school. *Bam!* You're in high school. *Bam!* You're in college. *Bam!* You have a job."

My dad was starting to bum me out. Because his list left out a lot of the fun parts in life, like going on vacation and riding your bike around during your free time. Before I could say anything, the warning bell rang. Some kids started jogging toward the building.

"Thanks for the Two-Taste Teton donuts!" I said as I climbed out of the car.

"Bessica, I want you to walk through those doors and have the best day of your life."

"Okay," I said. But even with my donuts, I didn't expect that to happen. I knew I'd have to wait until my spot was perfectly secure before I would have that kind of day.

As I hurried into the building, I kept looking left and right for the psycho-bullies. There were three of them: Cola, Beacher, and Redge. They were easy to spot because they were terrible-looking, mean, and fairly tall. *Look left. Look right. Left again. Right again.*

I made it to my locker and let out a breath of relief. But as I was turning my lock I saw something awful! Psycho-bully Cola's disgusting sneakers on his big feet.

"Hey," Cola said. "You've got Two-Taste Teton donuts."

I opened my locker and didn't say anything.

"Where did you get them?" Cola asked.

I didn't answer him. It was none of his business. I felt him hovering next to me. Even though I really hated how awful these psycho-bullies treated me, I still tried to stand up for myself. Except I did give psycho-bully Redge a pen every morning in nutrition. And I didn't do this out of generosity. I did it out of fear.

"I'll pay you for them," Cola said.

I shoved all my crud in my locker except my nutrition notebook, pencil box, and Two-Taste Teton donuts. Was I willing to part with my special snack? I liked the idea of earning some money. I slammed my locker and stood up.

"How much?" I asked.

But then Cola swiped my donuts right out of my hand.

"Sucker!" Cola said, and he turned around and ran off.

It was a very terrible feeling losing my Two-Taste Teton donuts. That was when I realized something that was a huge bummer. Becoming the school's grizzly bear mascot hadn't changed how psycho-bullies treated me. That wonderful dream I'd had of winning mascot and experiencing a complete social transformation, of finding my spot and landing a zillion cool friends, hadn't happened. I took a deep breath and looked down the crowded hallway. The truth was tough to face. But I was going to have to cheer my butt off before I experienced any social change. Faces blurred past me. Bodies bumped against me. Even though the hall was crammed full of people hurrying to class, I felt lonely. Outside myself it was noise, noise, noise, but inside things felt very quiet.

CHAPTER

The worst thing about school was that at times, it felt long and boring. Nutrition felt like that when our guest speaker, whose name was Ms. Leonard, discussed strategies for combating hypertension.

"Reduce dietary sodium. Limit your fried potato intake. Walk more."

And things didn't get any better when Mrs. Mounds reminded us of her expectations for our collages. "They must be thorough. A picture of everything that enters your mouth for two weeks."

"Even gum?" asked somebody in the front.

Mrs. Mounds nodded. "Even gum."

"Can we take pictures?" asked somebody in the middle.

"Yes," Mrs. Mounds said. "But try to find photographs in magazines and off food labels too. I want us to pay attention to how companies display and sell food to uninformed consumers."

I blinked at that. Was she calling our class a bunch of uninformed consumers? Maybe that was true of psycho-bully Redge. But not me. Except my mom did buy all the groceries and I rarely read the labels.

After nutrition, English felt long and boring when we took a comprehension exam about our permanent homework and I couldn't remember if the poem's fish was old or young. And math felt long and boring when we graded our homework in class and then continued to do mathy things. The one good thing about math class was that I sat next to an interesting person with dimples. Raya Papas. She also happened to be rude.

But I liked her anyway. In fact, I liked rude Raya Papas so much that right before the bell rang, I thought about asking her to Sylvie's birthday party. I doodled a roller skate on my notebook paper. Maybe deep, deep down, Raya wasn't that rude. Maybe math was such a cruddy experience for her that it turned her into a jerk for fifty-two minutes every day. Maybe if we met outside of math we'd get along really well. She looked over at me and saw me looking at her.

I sketched the date and time for Sylvie's party in big block letters. I also wrote the words DISCO/JUNGLE PARTY! Then I printed the name RAYA PAPAS on it. Then I tried to start a conversation.

"Hi," I said.

Then the bell rang for lunch.

"Bye," I said.

"Bye," Raya said, rolling her eyes at me. She sounded a little bored.

I gathered my things in my arms and walked down the hallway toward my locker. And then I got a good idea and I did something very brave. I stalked Raya all the way to her locker. And after she left, I slid the doodled invitation through a ventilation slot. I couldn't believe it. I'd invited Raya to Sylvie's disco/jungle party.

Then I hurried to my own locker to meet up with my lunch friends. I felt a little bit bad that I hadn't invited one of them to Sylvie's party. But it would have been hard to pick which one. I was lucky. I had a nice group of people to eat lunch with. Annabelle Deeter and her network of friends: Macy Wecker, Dee Hsu, and Lola Rodriguez.

Before I closed my locker, even though I didn't mean to, I thought of Sylvie. I unzipped my backpack's front compartment and pulled out my phone. I was excited to see that she'd left me another voice message and texted me again, but I was worried that I'd get caught listening to my voice mail in the hallway on a banned cell phone. So I just read my text very quickly.

Status check. Are you okay?

But since my principal problems were all her fault, I decided to leave Sylvie in the dark so she could worry more. I turned off my phone, then slammed my locker shut and drifted down the halls looking for Annabelle, Macy, Dee, and Lola. I usually found them near their lockers.

"Hi, Bessica!" Annabelle said. Then she ran up and hugged me, because that was how Annabelle liked to greet people. "You'll never guess what we learned about in social sciences."

She said this a lot when I saw her before lunch. I didn't take social sciences until next semester, so I was never able to guess what she'd learned about.

"We learned that during prehistoric times, dance was used as a form of communication and courtship!" Her eyes were very huge.

"Wow," I said.

"Isn't that wild? Next week we're going to watch a video about Neanderthals. Cool news! What if we learn their dance moves? I'll teach them to you and you can use them when you're the mascot!"

Then Annabelle started dancing in the hallway a little bit, which I did not enjoy. Plus, I didn't really need to learn Neanderthal dance moves, because my unique mascot talent was jumping rope. And if I needed to add some dance moves, Sylvie could teach them to me when I stopped being mad at her.

"Hi, Bessica!" Lola said. She flipped her long, dark hair over her shoulder and it made her silver earrings shake. Lola didn't give me a hug when she saw me. Ever. And that was okay. She was a very thin and serious girl who liked to wear a thick coat of lip gloss, which smeared easily.

"Did Annabelle tell you what we learned about in social sciences?" Lola asked.

I nodded. Sometimes it felt like I was taking an extra class. Because in addition to the six I took for grades, I also learned quite a bit about social sciences. Bleh. Macy and Dee walked up together looking cuter than usual. Macy had her curly red hair pulled back into a jumbo ponytail and was wearing a green shirt that made her green eyes look very bright. And Dee was wearing a puffy shirt that looked like something a pirate would wear, but somehow it also looked cool.

When they joined us they were both so happy that they bounced up and down a little and then we all walked to the cafeteria in a clump. I sort of dreaded our lunch conversations. Because unlike my conversations with Sylvie, which always involved stuff I wanted to talk about, Annabelle, Macy, Lola, and Dee liked chatting about fashion, and movies, and tap dance. And I didn't understand fashion. And I forgot movies after I watched them. And I'd only taken one summer session of tap dance with Sylvie and I tried not to think too much about that time in my life. Because back then Sylvie and I were so close we were like sisters. And there was a big part of me that wanted things to go back to that.

After we went through the lunch line we sat down and started eating what they'd put on our trays: boring ham and cheese sandwiches. This was unexpected, because we'd all chosen the hot lunch option. And everything on my tray felt pretty cold.

"What part of this is hot?" I asked.

"The cheese on the inside?" Lola said.

I took my top bread off and touched the cheese with my finger. It felt melted and room temperature. "Maybe at one time."

Everybody laughed at that. My lunch friends thought I had a pretty good sense of humor.

"Look! Look!" Annabelle whispered as she used her thumbnail to peel open her milk carton. Her voice was urgent and excited, which was normal for Annabelle. "Over by the napkins."

We all craned our necks to look at the napkins.

"Don't all look at once!" Annabelle gushed. But she should have told us that first.

"It's Jasper!"

We all watched as Jasper Finch pulled out a giant wad of napkins.

"He must be a messy eater," I said. He took thirty times as many napkins as a normal person.

"He wraps his retainer in them," Annabelle said dreamily.

"Gross," I said. I was pretty thrilled that all my teeth were basically straight and I didn't have a biting disorder that required orthodontic intervention.

"We should probably stop staring at Jasper," Lola said. So we did.

"Have you talked to him yet?" I asked.

Annabelle and Jasper had three classes together: math, English, and social sciences.

"Not yet," Annabelle said. "But I'm thinking about pretending that I lost my English homework assignment so I can call him."

"Oh," I said. Then I thought of the advice my mom had given me. Even though I wasn't sure it was great, I decided to share it with Annabelle. "Maybe you should try talking to him like he's an adult. Tell him you enjoy his personality and spiky hair."

Annabelle stopped eating and stared at me like I was crazy.

"I'd rather die!" Annabelle said.

"That's terrible advice, Bessica," Lola said.

"Yeah," Macy said. "It's like you're trying to make Jasper run away."

Dee didn't say anything. But even in her silence she seemed to disagree with me. I didn't like hearing that my advice was terrible. So I stuck up for it a little bit.

"People like compliments," I offered.

Annabelle swallowed. "That may be true. But it's a lot more fun to crush on Jasper and spy on him and talk about him with you guys than get rejected by him in front of everybody in my English class."

"Oh," I said. But I didn't think Annabelle should talk to Jasper like he was an adult in front of other people, I thought she should pull him off to the side. So I defended my advice some more. "You should pull him into a corner or empty hallway or closet and then talk to him."

Annabelle stared at me again. "That's nuts!"

"Totally!" Macy said.

"That's the worst advice I've ever heard one person give another person," Lola said.

"Yeah," Dee said.

"Really?" I asked. Because after offering it and defending

it, this advice didn't feel like my mom's anymore. It felt like mine. And I thought it was really mature. "I think I give pretty good advice. I helped my grandma find a bunch of potential boyfriends."

They all stopped eating again.

"Your grandma dates?" Annabelle asked. "Weird."

I shook my head. "It's not weird. There's lots of interesting and attractive people online."

"Wait," Lola said. "You help your grandma *online date*?"

"I used to," I said.

"Wacky," Macy said. "My grandparents don't even own a computer."

"Did it work?" Annabelle asked. "Does your grandma have a boyfriend?"

I didn't want to talk about Grandma's maniac welder boyfriend named Willy while I ate. So I steered around him. "It worked great," I said. "If she wanted, she could have more than one."

"I just want Jasper," Annabelle said. Then she smoothed her hair behind her ear and leaned across the table toward me. "Be serious. What's your best advice?"

So I leaned across the table toward her, because it turned out that I really liked giving advice—it made me feel powerful and important. "Establish a connection."

"Ooh," Dee said.

Annabelle kept leaning forward. "How? *How?*" She sounded panicked.

"Like I said. Be straightforward and tell him you enjoy his personality and spiky hair."

"It seems so risky," Annabelle moaned.

"Wait," Macy said. "Don't you have a huge crush on your next-door neighbor? Have you tried any of this out on him?"

I didn't say anything. I had not actually tried any of this out on gorgeous Noll Beck.

Macy gasped. "She hasn't."

"Why don't you take your own advice first and report back," Annabelle said.

She made a good point.

"He is so stinking awesome-looking," Annabelle said as she nibbled on her bread crust and stared madly at the back of Jasper's head, now two tables away.

And then instead of talking about boys and crushes, my lunch friends launched into a not-so-thrilling conversation about perfume. This was something that happened a lot. And the worst part about this was it meant that everybody was about to pull out their perfume pages, which were a bunch of pieces of notebook paper stapled together that stank, because Annabelle, Macy, Lola, and Dee went to the mall on a regular basis and collected perfume sample sticks. And at lunch they liked to pull out these collected sample sticks and sniff and discuss them.

"Ooh," Annabelle said. "That smells like vanilla pudding."

"Try this one," Lola said, offering her perfume page to me.

I took a sniff, but it smelled like an old saddle, and I wasn't sure I should say that.

"What do you smell?" Lola asked.

"Um," I said. "It's hard to describe."

"I know! I know! It's got multiple tones," Lola said. "But which one do you think is the overriding scent?"

That was a good question.

"Smell it again," Lola said.

But my head was already hurting, and so I really didn't want to suck more terrible fumes toward my brain. But I did it anyway, because I didn't want to offend my lunch friends. I took in a big breath.

"Okay," Lola said. "What's the first thing you smell?"

And so I answered very quickly.

"The earth," I said.

"What?" Lola said. "Are you sure?"

I opened my eyes. "Yep."

"That's weird," Lola said. "Because it's not even a musk."

I looked sympathetically at her and her perfume page.

"I think I'm going to buy Garden Spring Breeze," Macy said. "I'm ready to have a signature scent."

"No way!" Annabelle said, coughing on her milk in surprise. "I want one too."

I wasn't sure that was a good move. Grandma Lefter once told me that the world was changing and people were wearing perfume less and less in an attempt to smell as inoffensive as possible.

"I want to smell like a waterfall," Annabelle said.

"Ooh," Dee said.

"So cool," Macy said.

I just ate my sandwich. Until Annabelle said something that got my attention. "Why is Alice Potgeiser staring at you like she hates you?"

"Huh?" I said.

I looked over at the cheerleading table and Alice was glaring right at me. Ever since she'd failed to beat my butt for mascot and we'd tied, she'd been acting very hostile toward me. Mainly just by looking at me with disgust.

"She thinks she's so cool because she can do backflips, but so can monkeys," Lola said.

"Yeah," Dee said.

"She's a lame-o," Macy said. "And I'm glad she hurt her wrist and has to wear that stupid brace on it."

"Shhh," I said. I didn't want Alice to know that my friends and I compared her to monkeys. And before I could shush my lunch friends again or make my own quiet monkey comparison, a hand landed on my shoulder and I jumped a little. Because I wasn't used to hands touching me during lunch. I looked up. It was our school secretary, Mrs. Batts.

"Your mother is in the office," she said.

Annabelle, Macy, Lola, and Dee looked at me with interest and concern.

"It's about the mascot uniform," I said. I hurried to explain as fast as I could, because I was a little bit worried Mrs. Batts might mention my foot fungus. As I stood up and dumped my tray and left the cafeteria with Mrs. Batts, EVERYBODY looked at me. Even Alice and her cheerleader friends and the psycho-bullies. I was very disgusted when I saw Cola, Beacher, and Redge eating my Two-Taste Teton donuts. I wanted to focus on my shoes and the ground. But I thought that might make me look like I'd done something wrong. So I smiled and carried the rest of my ham and cheese sandwich in an unworried and happy way.

My mom was sitting in a chair in the school office.

"I thought you'd spring me out of public speaking," I said. Because I thought that was the time my mom had said.

"This worked better for me," she said.

I didn't mention that getting out of public speaking would have worked better for me.

"Principal Tidge will be out in a minute," Mrs. Batts told us.

While we waited, Mrs. Batts sat at her desk sorting papers and stapling them in a really intense way. Every time she smacked the stapler shut with her hand, my mom jumped a little. I tried to make my mom feel more comfortable by talking about my classes with her.

"In nutrition today, we learned that Americans don't have a good understanding of portion size. We should only eat lean meat that's this big," I said, holding up my fist.

My mother looked at my fist.

"Mrs. Lefter," Principal Tidge said. She stood in front of her open door, wearing a very well-ironed ugly suit and smiling huge. "Sorry to keep you and Bessica waiting."

I followed my mom into the principal's office. As soon as she shut the door I saw the furry bear suit. It looked way more awesome than I had thought it would. It was a honey-brown color and the fur looked incredibly soft. I wanted to rub my face in it right then and there. But I held back.

"Here's some information about the upcoming mascot clinic," Principal Tidge said, handing my mom a piece of paper.

"Wow," my mom said. "A six-hour class in mascot etiquette."

"Sometimes it only lasts five hours," Principal Tidge said. "All mascots in the district are asked to attend. It gives the mascots a chance to meet each other and learn new cheers."

"Awesome!" I said.

"At the clinic you and Alice will need to take turns wearing the suit," Principal Tidge explained.

That wasn't ideal, but it was okay. "The suit looks great!"

"Thank you," Principal Tidge said. "I picked it out. And interestingly enough, and lucky for you, we have a choice in mascot footwear."

I was very intrigued to learn about my choices.

"They accidentally sent us two sets of hind paws. We were going to send one back, but considering Bessica's foot condition, I think it makes more sense to let her and Alice each have their own pair of paws for the season.

"Since you were unable to make the meeting, and since Alice and I and Mrs. Potgeiser divvied up the schedule, I figured it made sense to let you choose which pair of paws you wanted."

"That does make sense," I said, nodding.

"Since it's shared, the costume has to stay here," Principal Tidge said. "But if you'd like, you can take your paws home. I imagine it would be helpful to practice jumping rope while wearing them."

"Yes!" I said. "It would."

"About Bessica's foot condition," my mother interrupted.

"It's getting much better," I blurted out. "I caught it early and I'm using special cream."

"No need to tell me the details," Principal Tidge said. "These things happen."

"Actually—" my mom started.

But I cut her off. "Next time I go to the public swimming pool, I will not go barefoot!"

Knock. Knock. Knock.

"Yes?" Principal Tidge said.

Mrs. Batts poked her head in the door. "I just caught the head of custodial services. You said you needed to speak with him."

Principal Tidge stood up. "I did."

"That's cool," I said. Because I sort of wanted her to leave before my mom could say anything truthful.

"Bessica, I've printed out the schedule. It's right here." She handed it to me. "All your games are highlighted. Boys' football. Boys' basketball. And Track and Field Days."

"Ooh," I said. I didn't realize I'd get to perform at Track and Field Days.

"Your first game is in two weeks. You'll be cheering against T.J. the Snake River Tiger."

"I'm cheering against T.J. the Snake River Tiger?" I asked. "I thought Alice wanted to cheer against him."

"She's cheering against the wildcat," Principal Tidge said.

That was right. I had mixed up my big cats.

"Mrs. Batts has both pairs of hind paws, and she'll let you choose which one you want," Principal Tidge said. "Sorry to run out on you, Mrs. Lefter. But we have a ventilation issue."

And then, before my mom could object, Principal Tidge was gone and Mrs. Batts entered the office holding up one pair of furry, fluffy, awesome paws with claws, and one pair of dingy-looking paws that looked like they'd already been used.

"You should probably use these," my mom said, pointing to the cruddy paws. "They'd be easier to jump rope with."

I shook my head. "But these look like actual bear paws."

I took them from Mrs. Batts and stuck them on my hands. *"Roar!"* I said to my mom. I was so thrilled.

Mrs. Batts laughed at me. "Great choice." Then she turned around and left the room.

"Bessica Lefter, I am beyond uncomfortable with what just happened here," my mom said.

"I know," I said. "But after she offered me my own set of take-home paws we really didn't have a choice." I reached up and touched my mom gently on the shoulder with one of my terrifying paws. "Grandma is going to love these."

This made my mom smile a little bit. Because we both missed Grandma. Neither one of us brought up how stupid it was that she left us to go on a road trip in a Winnebago with her new boyfriend, Willy. Stupid Winnebago.

"Bessica?" a soft voice called.

I flipped around to see who it was. Half of Lola's head peeked through the doorway.

"Hi, Lola!" I said. "This is my mom and these are my bear paws."

Lola peeked the rest of her head through the doorway and waved very politely at my mom. "I was just checking on you. I'm going to go back to the cafeteria."

"Thanks!" I said. "Tell everyone I'm cool and I was just getting my paws."

Lola nodded.

"Nice meeting you, Lola," my mom said.

"I eat lunch with her," I explained. "She's a very serious person. Also, we're in PE together."

"You should invite her over," my mom said.

"Ooh," I said. "Can we eat junk food and watch bad

television?" Sylvie and I used to watch bad television and eat cheese puffs. I missed those days.

"Let's invite her over for a movie and pizza. Okay. I need to get back to work. Hand me the paws," my mom said.

But I sort of wanted to keep them.

"There's no way they'll fit in your locker," she said.

But I thought maybe I could just carry them around all day. My mom kept her hands held out.

"Fine," I said, handing them over.

"You better hope this grand moment of dishonesty doesn't come around to bite you in the butt," my mom said.

I was really surprised to hear her use the word *butt* in my principal's office. Besides, wasn't this all Sylvie's fault? Shouldn't she have been the one getting bitten in the butt?

I looked into my mom's worried eyes. "That will never happen," I told her. And when I said those words to her, I totally believed they were true.

"What do you have now?" my mom asked.

"Mr. Hoser," I said. "Geography." It sure would have been nice if my mom had just taken me home. I fluttered my eyelashes and smiled.

"You're not leaving school early," she said. "Have a great rest of your day."

Then she kissed me on the head and walked out. I followed her into the empty hallway and finished the last bite of my ham sandwich and then almost gagged. Because Alice Potgeiser came rushing up to me.

"Which paws did you pick?" she asked. She was breathing heavy and looked upset. Then she poked her head into Mrs. Batts's office and saw the cruddy paws still on her desk. She turned and looked at me like she wanted to stab me with a pencil. And this worried me, because the school office had a ton of those. "Are those mine or yours?"

"Yours," I said. And inside I was laughing a little bit in delight, because I'd gotten the superior mascot footwear. *Ha, ha, ha.*

"Fine," Alice said. "Take the better paws. It doesn't matter."

"I'm glad you feel that way," I said. Even though I knew she thought it mattered a great deal.

"You're such a nickel," Alice said.

I just looked at her like I didn't know what she was saying. Because I didn't.

"It means you have very little value to me. Or anyone."

I tried to think of a comeback. "I like nickels."

Alice rolled her eyes. "You would." Then she cleared her throat and smiled at me in an evil way. "Also, I should probably tell you that your mascot career is over."

I gasped. Was it possible that Alice knew about my faked foot fungal infection?

"Yeah, I made it so you'd be cheering against the most vicious mascot during your first game," Alice said.

But that didn't sound so bad to me, because I thought me and the other mascot could maybe put on the best show ever.

"You'll look like a dweeb. And T.J. will look like a rock star. Because he's a pro and you're a nickel."

I considered reminding her that I liked nickels again, but I didn't. I was starting to feel worried that maybe I would look like a dweeb in front of the school.

"You act like you're special, but you're not," Alice said. "And everybody is going to be able to see that."

And when she said those words, they hit me hard. I worried that maybe there was a little truth to them. I wanted to be special and find my spot. And part of finding my spot meant that I wanted other people to think I was special too. From there I'd become majorly popular.

The bell rang, and Alice looked at me and leveled her brace-covered hand toward my heart.

"I don't know what sort of medical emergency you faked to get the good paws, but I'll get to the bottom of it. And when I do, everybody is going to know that you're a total sham."

I don't think anybody had ever called me this many

names in a row. *Nickel. Dweeb. Sham.* Alice didn't stick around for me to start calling her names. I was surprised that Alice was able to hurt my feelings so much, because I didn't even like her. But those names and their sharp corners kept tumbling around inside me. *Nickel. Dweeb. Sham.* And just when I thought my feelings couldn't be hurt any worse, I heard Alice say the following terrible things after she turned the corner.

"Of course I'd like a Two-Taste Teton donut! Mmm, mmm, mmm. Thanks, Cola. These flavor flecks rock!"

CHAPTER

When your life is going terribly, it's pretty easy to have nightmares. That night I dreamed something so horrific and rotten that it made me sweat in my sheets. In my nightmare, I was stuck on the ledge of a building. And nobody would help me get down. And there was scary wind blowing and crazy birds flying and I was terrified. Plenty of people walked past with ladders: Annabelle Deeter, Sylvie, the gorgeous Noll Beck, Mom, Dad, even Grandma Lefter!

But whenever I yelled at them to get me a ladder, they all said the same thing. "You found your way up there.

You can find your way down." Even Grandma told me that. Which I couldn't believe! Because standing on the ledge of a building is totally unsafe. Then Sylvie walked past and she had the best ladder ever. So I yelled, "Sylvie, I'm stuck on a ledge! Help me!" And she said, "You found your way up there. You can find your way down. Plus, you should have called me back!"

That was when I dream-yelled, "I'm sorry!"

And Sylvie dream-yelled back at me, "I bet you are, Fungal Foot!"

I popped my eyes open and stared into the darkness while I sweated and sweated and sweated. Holy crud. I had never expected Sylvie to treat me that way when I was stuck on a ledge. Then the hallway light flipped on.

"Are you having a nightmare?" my mom asked.

Even from my darkened room, I could see that she looked terrible. Her hair poufed where it was normally flat and was flat where it normally poufed. And she had white cream smeared all over her forehead and nose.

"You could tell I was having a nightmare?" I asked. Because that meant my mom was psychic and that freaked me out a little bit.

"I heard you yelling," she explained.

"Oh," I said. That made more sense than having a mom who suddenly became psychic in the middle of the night.

"Are you sleeping with your bear paws?" my mother asked.

I blinked at her. Then I reached above my head toward the area of my bed I referred to as my pillow zone and felt my bear paws and their glorious fur.

"Your scalp oil will damage their fluffiness," she said.

I sat straight up and removed the bear paws from my pillow zone. My mother had never mentioned that I had fluff-damaging scalp oil before.

"What was your nightmare about?" she asked.

"I was stuck on a dangerous ledge," I said. And when I told my mom this, I remembered how alone and afraid I had felt up there and my voice got shaky. "And nobody would help me get down."

My mother walked into my room and sat down beside me. "But you're not on a ledge. You're safe in your bed."

"I know," I said. "But in my dream nobody walking past would help me. Not you or Dad or Sylvie or Grandma. And you all had excellent ladders."

My mother leaned down and kissed me on the forehead. "I'm going to tell you a secret."

But I wasn't too excited to hear it. Because my mother's secrets were usually pretty lame and actually sounded like messages you could find inside fortune cookies.

"It's a good news secret," she said.

That sounded better. "What is it?"

"Grandma is coming home early to surprise you," she said.

What? What? What? I grabbed at my heart and screamed. This was the best secret my mom had ever told me.

"When?" I cried.

"Calm down," my mother said. "We have a few days."

"No way! A few days? We need to make preparations." My mind raced with things to do.

"No. We need to go back to bed," my mom said softly as she pulled the blanket toward my chin.

"Are we going to make her a special dinner?" I asked. "I know! We can order her favorite dinner from the new Thai restaurant in Rexburg!" Grandma had never eaten there, and one thing Grandma always did was eat at new restaurants as soon as they opened in Rexburg.

"We can talk about this in the morning."

"Oh!" I yelled. I'd thought of something else, and I didn't want to talk about this in the morning, I wanted to talk about it right now. "We need to clean up her room!" My mom and dad had put some boxes in her room in the basement, and we shouldn't make Grandma live with boxes. "And!" I yelled, because I'd thought of something else. "We need to make Dad go down there and kill all the big spiders." Because we shouldn't make Grandma live with those either.

I felt my mom rubbing my back. "We'll talk about it over breakfast." Then the hallway light flickered. I looked at the light switch. My dad was doing that.

"What's all the yelling about?" my dad asked. "Did you have a nightmare?"

I sighed. My dad was very behind in what was happening in my bedroom. "Yes," I said. "I was stuck on a ledge and nobody would give me a ladder. Not even you." I pointed at him when I said this. "But then Mom came in and told me that Grandma is coming back in a few days. Hey. Maybe you should go downstairs and kill the spiders right now while they're still sleeping."

My dad yawned. "It's bad luck to kill spiders."

But I didn't really care. Because they frightened me.

"We're not going downstairs in the middle of the night," my mom said. "We're all going to go back to bed."

But I felt very wide awake.

"What time is it in Minnesota?" I asked. "Maybe I could call Grandma and ask what she wants to eat for her homecoming dinner!" I reached for my phone, but my mom stopped me.

"It's the middle of the night there, too," my mom said.

"Bummer." Then I laid my head back down on my pillow zone.

"I think we should turn off the light," my mom said.

Click.

"But I'm not tired," I said. I closed my eyes. I felt my mother stand up.

"I'll always give you a ladder, Bessica," my dad said.

That felt good to hear.

"Me too," my mom said. "And so will Grandma."

"And even Willy," my dad said.

"Willy!" I shot back up. The guy who had showed up in a stinking Winnebago and taken Grandma away and ruined everything? I basically hated him.

"Willy will be coming with Grandma," my dad said.

"I wasn't going to mention that part," my mom said.

"I just figured Grandma would leave Willy in New Mexico where he belongs and come home to us," I said. My stomach felt like it was tying itself into terrible knots.

My mother turned on the hallway light again. "But Grandma and Willy are a couple now."

What? How? Why? Ugh. This didn't make any sense. "No!" I screamed.

"Don't yell, Bessica. You're going to wake yourself back up again."

"Dad already woke me back up when he told me the worst news ever!" I stabbed my finger in his direction again.

"We'll talk in the morning," my mom said.

Click. My room went dark again.

I'd woken from my ledge nightmare only to enter a much worse one. Willy was coming to my house. Because Willy and Grandma were a couple. What was wrong with Grandma? Why would she want to be a couple with that guy? Why didn't she want to stay a family with us?

Willy. Willy. Willy. I couldn't get him or his cowboy hat and head out of my mind. I knew that at one point I'd made a promise to Grandma to like him, but I'd changed my mind. And I had every right to do that. Because when I told Grandma I would like Willy, I didn't know they'd become a couple and return from their road trip *together*. Bleh.

I reached over and picked up my phone to see what time it was. It was 3:21 a.m. Then I saw that Sylvie had left me a bunch of messages. I had a whopping seven new Sylvie messages. It wasn't like me to let my messages pile up like that. I must've been a lot angrier with Sylvie than I'd realized. Since I was already up and feeling miserable, listening to Sylvie apologize to me over and over seemed like a smart way to spend the middle of the night.

Saturday

This is crazy! Did Principal Tidge get in touch with your mom? Are you okay? Call me back and tell me everything! I'm so sorry.

Saturday

Are you okay? What's going on? Why aren't you texting me back? You need to call me right away so I can stop worrying.

Sunday

I'm going to bed soon. But I'll be up for another hour. Are you mad? Is that why you're not responding? Please don't be mad at me. I didn't mean to cause you any mascot problems. I'm really very sorry.

Sunday

No message. Just a dial tone.

Sunday

I still haven't heard from you. This is getting annoying.

Monday

Do you just expect me to keep calling and texting you every day and never hearing anything back? You're being mean to me. I said I was sorry.

Monday

I'm done. This isn't how you treat your friends, Bessica. I'm giving you an ultimatum. Either you call me back tonight, or we're officially not friends. And that means no coming to my birthday party. For real.

I looked at my clock. It was too late to call. But it wasn't too late to text. I thought really hard about what I should say.

> **Me:** What you did was awful. I'm not over it.

I held my phone to my chest. I felt much better after I sent that. Sylvie should feel bad for a couple of more days for what she did.

> **Sylvie:** You should learn to forgive.

I was very surprised that she was still awake. I thought of something else to text.

> **Me:** Think about my feelings. Not yours.
> **Sylvie:** It's always about you.
> **Me:** Shut up!!
> **Sylvie:** You are so bossy!
> **Me:** You terrible friend!
> **Sylvie:** You too!!

And that last text arrived so quickly that it made me think that Sylvie didn't care about me at all. So my next text to her was a real zinger that came right from my wounded heart.

Me: You have elf ears!! Ha!

I sent her that because when we both got our matching pixie haircuts at the beginning of the year, the worst part of her cut was that it revealed her triangular ears. They looked so pointy that Sylvie cried, and the stylist used a ton of hair spray to try to cover them back up. But that didn't look so hot.

I waited for Sylvie to text me back. And I waited. And I waited. What was she thinking? I stared at the glowing blue display of my phone. Because I hadn't touched a button in over a minute the display went gray. I touched a button to turn it blue again. And then I made a terrible realization. I hated fighting with my Sylvie. And I worried that last message might have been too mean. I scrolled through my other texts. They all seemed mean. What had I been thinking? Did being awake in the middle of the night turn me into a mean person?

I didn't text Sylvie anymore. I just stayed very still and held my phone. I wondered if she felt bad too. I wondered if she'd text me tomorrow. I wondered if maybe she'd wake up and forget that all this rude texting even happened.

WAYS TO MAKE THINGS WAY WORSE IN MIDDLE SCHOOL

1. Learn lame cheers
2. Become caged
3. Adopt a lizard
4. Go to parties uninvited
5. Lack battle plans

CHAPTER

We were late, and this was terrible. Plus, going to another middle school's gym sort of frightened me. I didn't know what to expect. Both of my parents rushed me down the hallway.

"Flat Creek Middle School is a maze," my mother said.

"When I went to school, where this building stands used to be a cheese store," my dad said.

When it came to middle school, my dad was a very nostalgic person.

"Did you ever buy cheese here?" I asked.

"No," my dad said. "Way too expensive. But a couple of times I sampled their free curds."

My mom kept reading the directions for how to find the school gym. But it didn't work, and we ended up at a closed gate outside the cafeteria.

"I really don't want to be late," I said. "I want to have time to put my paws on my feet and walk around and get acclimated."

Even though I should have been super-excited about meeting the other mascots, I felt a little uneasy. I wasn't sure how to act around them. Would we high-five each other? Or share crazy cheers? Or maybe we'd be rude and growl. I just wasn't sure.

"These directions are useless," my mother said. "They say we need to go to the south section of the school and find the east wing. I didn't know I was supposed to bring a compass."

"Shhh," my dad said. "Let's listen for noise."

We all shushed and listened very carefully. We heard faraway squeaking and cheering.

"This way," my dad said, pointing left.

As soon as my dad pointed out the correct direction, I started running. Fast.

"Slow down, Bessica," my mom said.

"I can't be late!" I said. Because another fear I had was that Alice Potgeiser would arrive before I did and turn all the other mascots against me. And that fear wasn't a crazy fear. That was basically what was going to happen if I was late.

It only took me two minutes of running before I made it to the gym. The green metal door was propped open with a chair and a bucket. I looked inside the bucket and it was full of rocks.

I walked into the gym and saw my worst fear coming true: Alice was there, and she was in the middle of all the mascots. It looked like she was trying to teach them how to do standing backbends. Ugh.

"Bessica!" my mom said as she ran up behind me. "I want to let the supervisor know that we'll be picking you up when you're finished."

"Who's your supervisor?" my dad asked in an excited voice. "Is it Ms. Penrod?"

Ms. Penrod was my PE teacher, who also happened to be a former Olympian. Also, she and I had a little awkward history.

"Ms. Rich is our mascot advisor," I said. "She wears a lot of spandex."

I saw her across the gym and pointed.

"Isn't she standing next to Ms. Penrod?" my mom asked.

I nodded. My mom had already met all my teachers.

I gave my dad a quick look. "Please don't say anything about the size of her arms." Because they were huge.

"I'd never do that," my dad said. Then he started moving in her direction. And I followed.

"Bessica Lefter!" Ms. Penrod said as we walked up to her. "Nice paws."

I lifted them up so she could get a better look. That was when I noticed Alice Potgeiser getting into the bear mascot suit. That didn't seem fair! We were supposed to share it.

"Hey," I said. "Why does Alice get to wear the bear suit?"

Ms. Penrod and Ms. Rich glanced at Alice. A student dressed like a falcon was zipping her up.

"We only have one grizzly bear costume, Bessica. You're going to have to share," Ms. Rich said.

"Bessica is great at sharing," my mom said.

I frowned. "Why does she get it first?" I was worried that she'd never take it off. And then I'd look like the mascot who didn't belong.

"She was here first," Ms. Penrod said.

I looked up at my mom and her stupid map.

"You've got your paws," my dad said.

But I hadn't even gotten a chance to wear the suit for longer than two minutes. I really wanted to put it on.

"We'll be finishing around three o'clock," Ms. Penrod said. "Mrs. Dudley will be supervising the clinic. She'll be teaching the basics and throwing in some advanced techniques."

I looked around for Mrs. Dudley. I hoped she'd teach me a bunch of advanced techniques. Because I didn't care about average techniques.

"First things first," Ms. Rich said. "You need to join a group. For today's clinic you're working in groups of three, since you'll need two spotters. The eagle and spud still need a member."

I looked at the eagle and spud. I was sort of hoping to get teamed up with a vicious mascot so I could learn the most. What would I learn by working with a bird and a vegetable? Not much. And what was a spotter?

"Is that spud costume made out of foam?" my dad asked. "It looks fantastic."

"Mascot material has come a long way. Take a look at the tiger," Ms. Rich said.

I glanced at the tiger. This was the person I would be cheering against in my first game. Oh no! His stripes were sparkly—they looked like they were made out of glitter. And he really knew how to whip his tail like a maniac. *Swish. Swish. Swish.*

"Mascots with tails have an advantage," I mumbled.

"What?" my mom asked.

I didn't elaborate or repeat my observation. I just

tried not to think about how nervous I was about cheering at my first game and distracted myself by looking around.

"All right, sunshine," my dad said. "I expect to see a new cheer tonight when you get home."

"Okay," I said, even though I thought that was a dumb thing to tell me. Because any cheer I did for him would be a new cheer. He'd never seen me do one.

"Bye," I said. I was ready for them to leave. But they stood and watched me.

"See you later," I said. They still didn't move. And I didn't move. Why wasn't I moving?

"Don't be nervous," my mom said. "Meeting new people is awkward for everybody."

"They're as scared to meet you as you are to meet them," my dad said.

"I'm not scared," I said. I wandered toward my group. What do you say when you approach a person who looks like a baked potato?

I began waving at the spud and the eagle way before they even started looking at me, which made me feel a little bit like a dweeb. The spud was showing the eagle how to do backward somersaults. I sure hoped bears didn't have to do those.

"There's no way I can do that with my beak," the eagle said.

"What about this?" the spud suggested. Then he did something that looked like break dancing.

"I'd lose a ton of my plumage," the eagle said.

"Yeah," I said, finally pushing myself to speak. "You'd make a bald spot."

"Well, I am an eagle," the boy said as he took off his eagle head.

The good thing about his appearance was that he looked like a nice person. He had blond hair and big straight teeth. The bad thing was he had two zits. And it was hard not to stare at the big one on his nose.

"Are you Bessica?" the eagle asked. "I'm Duke. And this is Pierre. He's a potato."

I was surprised that Duke and Pierre already knew who I was. It made me feel a teensy bit famous and my skin goose pimpled.

"You've already heard about me?" I asked.

"Of course," Duke said. "Alice came around and told us all about you."

I could feel my face turning red. I knew I should say something quickly to regain a good reputation. But I didn't know what. I hoped she hadn't told them I was a nickel!

"Alice doesn't even know me!" I said. "Don't believe anything she told you."

Duke and Pierre looked at each other in a confused way

and then looked back at me. "She said that you were co-mascots."

"Oh," I said. "Well, that's true."

"You missed this assignment," Pierre said. "Before we start the clinic we're supposed to come up with a cheer as a way to introduce ourselves."

"Really?" I asked. Because I thought I should be taught *how* to cheer before that happened.

"Do you have any music?" Duke asked.

I shook my head.

Pierre smiled. "That's okay. You don't have to have music. Some mascots like to create a theme song and enter the performance arena while it plays."

"That sounds cool," I said. My mind starting racing to find grizzly bear songs. But none came to me.

"I don't have a theme song," said Pierre. "Because I think it runs counter to being a potato. We are simple vegetables. Tubers, actually."

"Right," I said. We'd learned that in nutrition.

"Looks like you're not going to have a costume for the first half," Duke said, "so you should probably just work on moves."

I glanced around the room. All the other mascots seemed to already be practicing stuff. I think that Pierre could tell that I was nervous.

"Is this your first clinic?" Pierre said.

I nodded.

"Do you want us to show you our introductory cheers first?" Pierre asked.

"Yes, please," I said. Maybe it was a good thing I hadn't gotten paired with a vicious mascot. Because Pierre and Duke were very helpful.

"Here's mine," Duke said. "We take our heads off for the introductory cheer. Because we need to chant and a mascot never does that with his head on. You knew that, right?"

"You want to reduce vocal strain," Pierre said pointing to his neck. "Over time your throat will develop painful nodules."

I nodded like I knew that. But I actually had no idea.

I watched as Duke jogged in place and flapped his feathered arms. "We run. We block. We fly. So high." He took a breath and kicked face-level at the audience two times. "Flat Creek Eagles take the win. Victory or die!" Then he released a high-pitched bird cry that made me cover my ears.

"So we don't say our names in the introductory cheer?" I asked. Because I thought that was the main reason we were introducing ourselves.

"No," Pierre said quickly. "As a mascot, your identity should be fused with your team."

I thought about my school's team. Did I want my

identity fused with them? I guessed it was too late to feel differently.

"My turn," Pierre said.

"Hit high! Hit low. Let's go, Potato!"

Pierre's cheer might have been short. But he repeated it three times. And each time he finished, he did a forward or backward somersault and jumped to his feet again.

"Don't you get dizzy?" I asked. Because I thought I would.

"The trick is to close your eyes," Pierre said.

"Okay," Duke said. "Show us what you have."

I thought back to my cheer that I'd performed to win half mascot. I'd used a jump rope and skipped around the gym with it, mostly shouting, "I'm a bear!" I'd sweated so hard my pants had slipped off and I accidentally flung them onto the crowd and Ms. Penrod's head. I didn't want to do that again. So I thought up a short cheer and yelled, "Bear! Bear! Win!"

And I grabbed my jump rope out of my bag and yelled, "I'm a bear!" And I jumped rope a few more times and then I stopped and released a bunch of power kicks. It bummed me out when one of my mascot paws flew off my foot and hit Pierre in the face.

"Whoa," Duke said. "Careful."

"Sorry," I said. Then I put my paw back on my foot.

Pierre and Duke looked at each other. "Do you want some friendly advice?" Duke asked.

"Sure," I said.

"Don't do that as your introductory cheer," Duke said.

This made me feel terrible. But I didn't tell them that. I decided to follow the advice of my speech teacher, who said you could always locate ways to improve if you focused on your strengths.

"What was the best part of my cheer?" I asked.

Pierre looked at his brown spud feet, and Duke looked at the ceiling.

After some silence, Duke finally said, "It's definitely good that you mentioned you're a bear."

There was more silence.

"Have you ever watched a bear?" Pierre asked.

I couldn't believe I was being judged so harshly by a potato.

"Think of it this way," Duke said. "In my cheer I brought eagle attitude. And Pierre brought potato personality. That's the whole trick of being a mascot. You have to bring it."

"And be more bear," Pierre said.

I wanted to tell Duke and Pierre that I already knew that. But I didn't feel like defending myself. I heard Alice Potgeiser's voice exploding at the other end of the gym.

"Who dat? Who dat? Yell it! Sell it!" I watched as Alice

did a series of high kicks in the bear suit. It looked a little funny to watch furry legs move like that, but it also looked very amazing. "We're the best! From the west! Yell it! Sell it! Bear! Bear! Bear!"

"She's good," Duke said.

"Real good," Pierre said.

It disappointed me that they were right.

Ms. Rich came by with a handout that listed all our games and the times we needed to arrive in our costumes on the field. Instead of working more on my introductory cheer, I decided to go and read the list and maybe eat a snack.

I moved off to the sidelines and sat next to my backpack. Being a mascot was difficult. And also sort of a bummer.

Buzz. Buzz. Buzz.

Oh. I'd forgotten I had my phone. I pulled it out. Wow! It was a new text from Sylvie. I guess our war of texts wasn't over after all.

Sylvie: Are you still mean?

I stared at the text. How could she call me mean? That was ridiculous. I could think of forty people who were much meaner than I was. So I texted her back.

Me: Are you still lame?

I held my phone and anxiously awaited Sylvie's response. I didn't think it would be good.

"No phones in the gym!" a voice called. I don't even know whose voice it was. I just got up and went into the hallway and walked around and watched my phone.

Sylvie: You used to be nice.

That was so low. I texted back a good response right away.

Me: Whatev.

I turned left and right and left again waiting for Sylvie's next text. It didn't arrive. So I texted something else.

Me: You act like you're 10.

Then I got the great idea to spell out the sound of a baby crying, so I sent that too.

Me: WAH! WAH!

I waited and waited. It's hard to be in a war of texts with somebody when they don't text back. I finally stopped walking when I realized I was in a kitchen. How had I gotten here? I walked past some stoves and refrigerators and ended up in the empty cafeteria. Out of curiosity I opened one of the refrigerators and saw giant containers of mayonnaise and mustard. And an enormous vat of chocolate pudding. Yum. Then I shut the door and noticed that my phone was out of range.

This wasn't good. I walked to the closed gate and shook it a little to see if it would open. But it wouldn't. Then I tried to follow my steps and get out of the kitchen. But every door I found in there was a closet. I felt very panicked. I couldn't miss my first mascot clinic!

Walk. Walk. Walk.

How had I even gotten in this place? There was no way out. "Hello? Hello?" I called. "I'm locked in the kitchen!" But nobody was around. I tried opening all the doors again. One of them had to lead to freedom. I finally found one that wasn't a closet. It led to a hallway. But when I went into the hallway, I was blocked by another locked metal gate.

I was pretty sure this was the direction I'd come from. Somebody must have come behind me and locked me in. A janitor? A lunch worker? Alice Potgeiser? Anything seemed possible. "Hello! Hello!" I yelled. "I'm here for the mascot clinic!"

But nobody answered me.

I wandered back into the kitchen. Maybe there was

an emergency phone. *Walk. Walk. Walk.* Nope. I tried to think of a good solution. Maybe I should start a fire and set off the smoke detectors! But then I would be locked inside a cafeteria that was burning down. I sat down at one of the tables and listened to the terrible silence. Far away I could hear the sounds of squeaking and cheering. Wouldn't somebody eventually come and look for me?

Maybe. But how long would that take? I stared at my bear paws. How had this happened to me? Was I trying to sabotage myself? No. That wasn't what had happened. It was the war of texts with Sylvie. That was how I ended up caged in Flat Creek's cafeteria.

I jumped up and ran to the front gate. Somebody would hear me if I shook it hard enough. "Hello! Hello!" I thought about what Pierre had said about throat stress causing nodules. Oh well. "Hello! I'm stuck!" I grabbed the gate with both hands and yanked on it.

Rattle. Rattle. Rattle.

Not only was I not learning anything useful at mascot clinic, I was freaking out.

"My name is Bessica Lefter and I am trapped!"

I felt myself crying and I let go of the gate. I sat down on the floor and buried my head in my hands. I was going to be so behind by the time I learned any cheers.

"You really are trapped," a voice said.

I looked up happily. Freedom. That was what this voice meant to me. I was going to be let out of the cafeteria cage. But then I realized the boy standing on the other side was probably a kindergartener and most likely didn't have the keys.

"Go get your mom and tell her I'm locked in the cafeteria," I said. I stood up and held my hands out in a pleading way.

"My mom isn't here," the boy said.

"Okay," I said. "Get your dad."

"I can't," he said.

"Why not?" I asked. I was beginning to worry that maybe this kid was an orphan and I was making him feel bad.

"I don't know where he is," the boy said. "My name is Cole. And I'm lost."

"Bummer," I said. But I still had a lot of hope. Because Cole wasn't trapped inside the cafeteria and I could send him to get help for both of us.

"Okay," I said. "I'm going to give you my phone and I want you to walk over to the end of that hallway so you can get in range. Don't turn any corners. And I want you to call my mom and tell her to come back to the school because I'm locked in the cafeteria."

"That's a big message," the boy said.

"You can do it!" I said.

I handed him my phone through the metal gate. "Do you know how to use a cell phone? Just press the green button."

"I know how to use a phone. I'm in first grade."

It seemed like it took forever for Cole to take my phone and walk to the end of the hallway. I heard him say what I'd told him to say and then he walked back.

"What did she say?" I asked.

"Nothing," he said. "I got her voice mail."

This was awful. "Okay," I said. "You need to call my dad. Hand me my phone and I'll dial his number."

"Maybe I should call my sister," Cole said. "She's in the school."

"Really?" I asked. I got excited that his sister might be a teacher who had keys to the metal gates.

"She's a mascot," he said. "Her name is Alice."

Ugh. I didn't really want Alice Potgeiser to know that I had locked myself in a cafeteria. But I couldn't stay in this cage any longer.

It only took a few minutes after Cole called Alice for a huge group of people to arrive. Ms. Penrod and Ms. Rich seemed very concerned. And Flat Creek's cheer coach, Mrs. Dudley, also seemed upset.

"How did this happen?" she asked.

"I left to send a text and ended up in the kitchen somehow, and then I couldn't get back out," I explained.

"Bessica! Bessica!" I looked up and saw my mother running down the hallway toward me.

"I'm okay now," I said. But that wasn't entirely true. Because I was still locked in the cafeteria.

"We need to get her out," my mom said.

"Right now!" my dad said.

Ooh. It was good to see my dad. I hadn't seen him running behind my mom. I figured if they couldn't find the keys, he'd insist on sawing me free.

"We've walkie-talkied the janitor and he's on his way," Mrs. Dudley said.

"Sorry about this," I said.

Alice covered her mouth. It looked like she was laughing at me. I wished she'd put the stupid bear head back on so I wouldn't have to look at her.

"Are you doing okay in there?" Ms. Penrod asked. "I bet one of the refrigerators has some snacks if you need them."

I thought back to the jars of mayonnaise and vat of chocolate pudding. "I'm good."

"As much as I hate to say it, we should probably head back to the gym and finish up the clinic," Ms. Rich said.

"I understand," my mom said. "We'll wait here for the janitor."

"Do you want my phone number in case you've got any mascot questions?" Duke asked.

"Mine too?" Pierre offered.

"Sure," I said.

So I loaded them into my cruddy out-of-range phone. Then everybody except my mom and dad left.

"It's neat that you made some friends," my mom said. "I think I know the eagle boy's mother."

"And the potato kid seemed nice too," my dad said.

"Whatever," I said.

I reached my arm through the metal gate and my mom held my hand until the janitor came.

"I knew one day this would happen," the janitor said.

That didn't make me feel any better.

"If this ever happens again," the janitor said, and he unlocked the gate and rolled it open, "keep in mind there is a fire exit inside the kitchen. It will set off the alarm if you open it. But it's better than being stuck in the cafeteria all day."

"Good information," my mom said.

Once I was out of there all I wanted was to go home.

"Do you want a treat for the ride?" my dad asked as we passed through town.

"No," I said. "The only thing I want is my bed. And maybe we should start getting the house ready for Grandma."

Grandma. Grandma. Grandma. I missed her so much. Having her back in my life would make everything feel one hundred percent better. I just knew it.

CHAPTER

7

"Grandma is going to refuse to live with us if we can't make her room smell better than this," I said.

My mother had her hair tied back in a ponytail and was using a soapy sponge to clean the walls.

"You're being so negative," my mother said.

"No," I said as I gave a prolonged spray of ocean-scented air freshener, "I am talking to you like we're both adults. And storing mothballs down here was evil."

My mother stopped sponging the walls. "If we didn't use mothballs our clothes would look like Swiss cheese."

"Mom," I said, releasing more air freshener, "Grandma's room smells so poisony that I think I'm going blind."

Preparing the house for Grandma was taking a lot more time and energy than I'd thought it would. Because in the weeks since she had left, her room had turned into a dump.

"What are these?" I asked. I'd opened Grandma's chest of drawers and encountered a weird plastic thing and a bunch of small glass jars.

"That's a canning funnel and my best jam jars," my mom said. "I'm considering making strawberry preserves for the holidays."

My mom had tried to can vegetables and make jam once before and she'd caused an explosion that scattered broken glass all over the kitchen floor. We hadn't been able to go barefoot in there since.

"Why did you put all this junk in Grandma's room? She was only going to be gone a few weeks," I said.

"Our house feels like it's shrinking. Our stuff has to go somewhere," my mom said. "And sometimes people's plans change. I don't think Grandma plans to live here forever."

I turned around and looked directly at my mother. "Sure she does. It's great here." I wagged the canning funnel at her to really grab her attention. Then I suggested, "I think we should throw this away."

"Grandma won't need all the drawers," my mom said. She'd started sponging the walls again.

I cleared my throat in disgust. "If we don't give Grandma all her space back she's going to think we love her less." And I wasn't kidding. That was exactly how I would have felt if I came back and found a canning funnel in my underwear drawer.

"Fine," my mom said, scrubbing the baseboard energetically. "Where do you suggest I put my supplies?"

I didn't miss a beat. "A garbage can."

"Bessica, this cleanup should be enjoyable. Don't be difficult."

I put my finger on the air-freshener nozzle and held it down hard. I wasn't being difficult. I was looking out for Grandma and her feelings. And her underwear.

"I think you've released enough ocean scent," my mom said. "Grandma has a very sensitive nose."

"I know. The mothballs are going to kill her."

"Okay. Okay. Okay," my mom said, standing up and dropping the sponge in a bucket. "We need a break."

"Sweet!" Because that meant it was getting very close to the time when Lola would be coming over to watch a movie and eat junk food with me. I raced up the stairs to get the cheese puffs. But I couldn't find them, even after I'd opened all the cupboards where they should have been.

"What happened to the cheese puffs?" I asked.

"When you make your food collage, aren't you going

to be embarrassed to have to put cheese puffs on it?" my mom asked.

"Not at all," I said.

"I have pickles and olives," my mom said.

"I don't want my nutrition class to think I eat pickles and olives. Those are weird foods."

"What are weird foods?" my dad asked as he walked into the kitchen and plopped down a box.

"Pickles and olives," I explained. "I don't want pickles in my collage."

"She wants cheese puffs," my mom explained.

"I hardly have any orange food," I said. "The puffs will look great."

"I don't believe this!" my dad said. "Isn't anybody going to ask what I've got in the box?"

He made a good point. "What's in the box?" I asked.

My dad tore it open, but inside was another box. It looked like it was something electronic. My mom gasped and covered her mouth.

"Buck," she said, sounding horrified. "I told you not to buy that!"

"This will save me time and worry!" my dad said.

I read the box: RADAR JAMMER.

"What is it?" I asked.

"It's illegal!" my mother said.

I was shocked to hear this. Because my dad wasn't a criminal.

"Only in certain states," he said.

He used a pocketknife to open the smaller box. Then he slid a black plastic device with a long cord onto the table.

"Honestly, Buck," my mom said. "How fast do you need to go?"

"This isn't for intentional speeding. It's for accidental speeding," he explained. He sat down at the table, unfolded the directions, and started reading like mad.

"I still don't know what that thing is," I said.

"It's a laser jammer," my mom explained. "So when your father speeds down the highway and a police officer zaps his car with a laser gun, the officer can't get an accurate reading of his illegal speed."

"Ooh," I said. That didn't sound legal at all. Especially the part where my mom said "illegal."

"This unit costs a third of what a ticket would cost," my dad argued.

"Don't speed. Problem solved," my mom said.

Ding-dong. Ding-dong.

"That's Lola," I said. "Can we not fight in front of her or talk about how we buy things in the mail and use them to break the law?"

"Of course," my mother said.

"I'll take this out to the garage," my dad said.

"I feel sick to my stomach," my mom said.

"Please don't puke," I said. I really wanted Lola to have a positive experience at my house.

Letting Lola enter my house felt very wonderful. Because she was the first friend since Sylvie who I'd invited over.

My mom had already talked to Lola's mom on the phone for a long time, so Mrs. Rodriguez hadn't had to come inside and learn about us when she dropped Lola off.

"Cool carpet," Lola said as she took off her shoes and scooted across it in her socks like an ice-skater.

Until she said that, I didn't even know I had cool carpet.

"Are you hungry?" I asked. "We have snacks."

"I love snacks!" Lola said.

"Hi, Lola," my mom said as she came into the living room to greet my friend. I was thrilled that she was carrying a family-size bag of cheese puffs.

"Let's see what's on TV," I said.

"Let's watch a movie," Lola said.

That sounded good. "Ooh, have you seen this one?" I asked. I watched as a horse ran out of a barn and thundered down a hill.

"I have," Lola said. "The horse dies."

"You're supposed to say 'spoiler alert' before you tell me things like that," I said. Because that was what Sylvie used to do.

I kept clicking through the channels. But nothing looked good. I paused on a show about goats.

"Farm animals are boring," Lola said.

Because we lived in an area surrounded by farm animals, I sort of agreed. *Click. Click. Click.* I was surprised I couldn't find a TV show about whales or dolphins. Usually there were lots on Sundays.

"Maybe we should do something else," Lola said.

I stopped searching for something on TV and tossed the remote onto the couch. "Do you want to look through my movies?"

"No." Lola rolled over onto her back. "I know. Why don't you show me some cheers you learned at mascot clinic?"

I wasn't in the mood to tell Lola how I'd gotten into a war of texts with Sylvie and ended up caged in Flat Creek's cafeteria.

"Maybe later," I said. "Is there anything else you want to do?"

Lola looked at me and her eyes twinkled in a mischievous way. "Yes!" she said.

"What?" I asked.

"It might freak you out," Lola said.

"Why? Is it illegal?" I asked. I think the laser jammer made me ask that question.

"No," she said in a whisper. "But it might be dangerous."

I worried that maybe I didn't know Lola as well as I had

thought I did. I held my breath and waited for her to tell me what it was.

"I want to meet your gorgeous neighbor, Noll Beck!"

That made sense. Because Noll was extremely good-looking and wonderful.

"Do you want to spy on him?" I asked. "Because that's something I try not to do during the middle of the day."

Lola's eyes twinkled again and she smiled, and then she laughed in a way that made the hair on my arms stand up. "I don't want to spy on him. I want to meet him."

"Right," I said. "But I don't even know if he's home."

"Call him," she said.

I had never called Noll Beck. And I wasn't sure why Lola wanted to meet him so badly. He was my crush. She shouldn't have a crush on him too. Didn't she have her own high school neighbors?

"Maybe later," I said.

"Maybe now!" Lola cheered.

Until now I'd thought of Lola as serious and a little reserved. This was a new side of her. I wasn't sure how I felt about it.

"What would I say?" I asked.

"Take the advice you gave Annabelle," Lola offered.

I couldn't remember it exactly.

"Talk to him like he's an adult and tell him how you feel about him," Lola said.

I didn't realize how terrible my advice sounded until Lola gave it to me.

"Yeah," I said. "I don't really feel like doing that."

Lola got on her knees and crawled to the television set and turned it off. Then she flipped around and gave me her serious face. "What if he likes you too?" Lola asked. "Wouldn't it feel awesome to know?"

"He has a girlfriend," I said.

"Are you sure?"

I felt myself nod.

"People break up all the time," Lola said. "When's the last time you saw them together?"

I shrugged. "A couple of weeks ago."

"Where's your cell phone?" Lola asked.

"In my room."

Lola was a very determined person. As soon as we got to my room she closed the door and said, "This is the most exciting thing I've done all month!"

It was flattering to be part of the most exciting thing Lola had done this month. I picked up my cell phone and dialed Noll's number. I'd loaded it into my phone almost as soon as I'd gotten it, because I'd secretly hoped that one day Noll would call me, and I didn't want to be surprised. I wanted to know it was him who was calling. I held my breath as I waited for him to answer.

Ring. Ring. Ring.
"Maybe he's sleeping," Lola said.

Gorgeous Noll: Hello.
Me: Hi, uh, this is Bessica Lefter.
Gorgeous Noll: Well, what's new on the menu?

I tried to think of something funny to say.

Me: Corn dogs?
Gorgeous Noll: Ha. That's cute. So what's up, neighbor?
Me: I was just calling to talk to you.

I glanced at Lola and she was smiling huge and giving me a thumbs-up sign.

Gorgeous Noll: That's funny.
Me: It is?
Gorgeous Noll: Yeah. Because I've been meaning to call you.
Me: You have?

I muted my phone very quickly and told Lola, "He said he's been meaning to call me."

"Put him on speaker!" Lola said.

But I shook my head and unmuted Noll.

Gorgeous Noll: Can you meet me on my front steps in five?
Me: Yes,
Gorgeous Noll: Great!

Click.

"Wow," I said. "That went really well."

"This is unbelievable!" Lola said.

But that offended me a little bit. Why couldn't Noll Beck's asking to meet me on his steps be believable?

"Put on better clothes!" Lola said.

I looked at my clothes. I'd wiped my hands on my jeans a few times, so there were orange finger marks on them from the cheese puffs. I ran to my closet.

"Wear your jeans with the big pockets," Lola said.

But I didn't have any jeans like that. So I told her that.

"You wore them Friday," Lola said.

Lola paid attention to which jeans I wore on which day? Weird.

So I put yesterday's jeans on and a black T-shirt, because Lola and I both agreed that black was more adult than any other color. Even brown. Lola said she'd wait for me in my room. My stomach flipped a million times as

I walked over to Noll's. My life was crazy. One day I get locked in a school cafeteria with my bear paws. The next I get invited to a gorgeous guy's house. *Crazy!*

Noll sat on his steps waiting as I walked up. Even though it was chilly outside, he was wearing shorts. I could see the toned muscles in his calves and thighs. His hair looked dark and shiny even from this far away. I waved. He waved. And my knees got very shaky.

"How are things?" Noll asked.

And because I knew I was supposed to talk to him like he was an adult, I filtered everything I said and made sure it sounded adulty before it left my mouth.

"Respectably well," I said.

Noll laughed at that. "Well, you're probably wondering why I wanted to talk to you."

"I figured you wanted to have a conversation," I said.

Noll laughed again. He really seemed to be enjoying himself. Yay!

But then he stopped laughing and took a deep breath and said, "I'm leaving."

I felt like puking. How could this happen? Grandma was just returning, and now my gorgeous neighbor who finally wanted to start having conversations with me was going?

"When?" I asked.

"In a couple of days," he said.

"Forever?" I asked. I sure hoped the answer was no.

"Two weeks," he said. "I'm going to Wyoming."

"That sounds awful," I said. Because I forgot to filter that comment.

"I'm actually really excited," he said. "I'm taking riding lessons."

That explained why I kept seeing him on a horse.

"The reason I called you is because my girlfriend and I broke up," he said. "It's been a ton of drama."

Suddenly, this moment was the best moment of my life. Noll Beck broke up with his girlfriend and he wanted to talk about it with me! *Me!*

"Sorry to hear about the drama," I said. And I also reached out and sympathetically patted his knee. And he didn't stop me or pull away. He just let me pat him.

"I need your help," he said.

"Anything," I said. "Anything." I continued patting him.

"Could you feed something for me while I'm gone?"

Hmm. I didn't remember Noll having a dog.

"My girlfriend was supposed to feed my pet lizard for me while I'm away," he said. "My parents have a trip planned, so they can't do it for me."

Hmm. I didn't actually like lizards.

"So it will really just be the long weekend that they're gone," he said.

"Anything," I said again. And I was surprised to hear myself say that word in this context.

"Her name is Bianca. She's a green anole and she eats live crickets."

"Gross," I said.

"It's not gross. She's a reptile."

But I thought being a reptile was gross too. Except I didn't say that. I wanted to talk about stuff that mattered. For instance, why did Noll break up with his girlfriend?

"Hey," I said. "Can I ask you a question?"

"Yeah, but I'll also type up a list of everything you need to know. I actually want you to feed the crickets vitamins before you feed them to Bianca. It's called gut loading."

My stomach felt queasy to learn this.

"Not about the lizard," I explained. I pulled my hand off his knee, because it felt like I might have been patting him for a long time. "Why did you and your girlfriend break up?"

Noll shook his head. "These things just happen, Bessica. You'll understand when you get older."

But I was old enough to understand right now.

"I've got to get packing," Noll said as he popped up to a standing position.

"Yeah," I said. "I should probably practice my mascot routine."

Since the mascots were usually seventh and eighth

graders, I thought that reminding Noll I was a mascot made me sound older than a sixth grader.

"When's your first game?" Noll asked.

"Next week," I said.

"Who do you cheer against?"

"T.J. the Tiger."

Noll's face stopped looking happy and started looking concerned. "That kid is nuts. You don't have to stand near him, do you?"

I shrugged. I thought maybe I did.

"Listen, T.J. is a little prankster dweeb who isn't above tripping or shoving or worse. You keep your eyes peeled during your game. And if something happens and you need help, you can call me."

"Even if you're at horse school?" I asked.

"Absolutely."

I watched gorgeous Noll Beck walk back into his house and slam the door. When was I supposed to pick up Bianca the lizard? It didn't matter. He had just given me permission to call him whenever I wanted. I wondered if that meant he wanted me to. I ran back to my room so I could tell Lola. Too bad Sylvie and I were basically no longer friends. She'd explode if I told her what had just happened.

Lola screamed when I told her that Noll had broken up with his girlfriend and wanted me to feed his pre-

cious lizard, Bianca. She said we needed to call Annabelle, Macy, and Dee *immediately*. Everybody freaked
out when they heard the news, except Dee, who stayed
basically calm.

Dee said, "Relationships require bargaining skills."

And I said, "Whatever. That relationship went kaput.
Yay!"

"Do you want to call Sylvie?" Lola asked me after we
hung up with Dee.

What a terrible thing to ask me. I stared at my carpet
and contemplated what to do.

"Is something wrong?" Lola asked. "Or do you see a
bug on your carpet?"

I looked at Lola and her serious face. "I don't see a bug
on my carpet." Then I decided I didn't need to hide anything from Lola. "I can't call Sylvie because we had a war
of texts and now we're not talking to each other."

"What's a war of texts?" Lola asked.

"I sent her a mean text. Then she sent me a stinking
mean text. And that happened a few times and I ended
up making fun of her ears and she stopped texting me,"
I explained.

"Sending mean texts makes you feel good for a few minutes, but then you have to live with the aftermath."

"I never had a friend who used the word *aftermath* before," I said. It made things feel very tragic.

"My mom never texts or sends emails when she's angry. She always sleeps on it," Lola said.

"I bet your mom has a lot of friends," I said, sounding a little regretful.

"Tons," Lola said.

When Lola left I had mixed feelings about everything. I regretted my rude texts. I regretted not having learned anything at mascot clinic. I regretted not making Mom take the funnel and jam jars out of Grandma's underwear drawer. I regretted my father's purchase of an illegal jammer. And I sort of regretted agreeing to feed a lizard named Bianca live crickets. Because what did *gut loading* mean anyway?

CHAPTER

8

We sat at our lunch table and picked through our macaroni and cheese entrees, trying to rid them of evil bacon flecks that were buried in the sauce. Nobody wanted to discuss gut loading crickets.

"That's the most disgusting thing I've ever heard," Macy said. Then she made gagging sounds.

"Do you think crickets feel pain?" Lola asked.

"They must," Dee said, sounding very sad.

"Maybe I can just feed his lizard lettuce," I said. "Don't lizards in the wild eat that?"

"I think they eat crickets," Annabelle said. "Let's change the subject."

Okay. I stuffed some noodles in my mouth. I was worried that I was eating orange food again. My collage needed to have lots of different colors. I needed to mix it up and be on the lookout for foods that were purple and blue.

"Have you guys noticed Jasper's new shoes?" Annabelle asked.

"Yeah," Lola said. "His feet are growing."

"I know!" Annabelle said. "He's getting taller too."

I was surprised that they kept track of which shoes Jasper wore. Did they keep track of which shoes I wore? Because I basically just wore the shoes Grandma got me before she left. I could change the tongues with a variety of colors so they would match anything I owned.

"Have you talked to Jasper yet?" I asked.

Annabelle shot me a scared look.

"I think that strategy works really well," I said.

Nobody could argue with me.

"I can't do it at lunch in front of people," Annabelle said.

"Don't you have your last class together?" I asked.

Annabelle nodded.

"Do it there!" Lola said. "It would be so exciting."

For a person who wore a serious face most her life, Lola sure did like excitement.

"What do I say?" Annabelle said. "I don't want to scare him."

"Don't be aggressive," Dee said. "No creature on earth likes aggression!"

Dee's parents were dog trainers, so she would know.

"No aggression is a good idea," I said. "But I'd also be nice and compliment him."

"Ooh!" Macy said. "Tell him you like his butt!"

I could not believe how loud Macy said that.

"Shhh!" Annabelle said. "If he heard that I'd die!"

Then the bell rang and we all had to go to our terrible classes. I groaned.

"What are you guys going to learn about in geography today?" Lola asked me as we walked down the hall.

"Something about the Arctic," I mumbled. Mr. Hoser had recently assigned us a collage in that class too. I was supposed to picture the Arctic and paste images on a big piece of poster board of what I'd expect to see when I got there. I found that topic zero fun to think about.

"And what's your next class?" Lola asked.

We stopped in front of my locker.

"Public speaking. We're analyzing a popular speech made by Julius Caesar," I said.

"Isn't he dead?" Lola asked.

I bent down and started turning the dial on my

combination lock. "Yeah. A long time ago. A group of his friends stabbed him."

"Living in the olden days would've been a total drag," Lola said. "See you in PE."

Time dragged and dragged until it was time for PE. Sadly, even though I was liking Lola more and more, I didn't get to spend too much of PE with her. Since I'd won grizzly bear mascot, that class operated a little bit differently for me. I only had to do what the class was doing for the first half of the period. Then I got to go off to the side and practice my routine.

After I changed into my official PE uniform—a yellow T-shirt and purple pants—I sat on a bench in the gym next to Lola. But we didn't spend too much time talking, because Ms. Penrod took PE very seriously.

"Today we are going to test your abdominals," Ms. Penrod said.

I hated tests.

"We're going to learn ten ways to strengthen your abs!"

Strengthening my abs seemed better than jogging, so I didn't mind.

"But before we do that," she said, "let's jog around the gym five times to get our blood flowing. I'll set the pace."

There was a little bit of groaning when Ms. Penrod said this. Because her pace was very, very fast. I stood up and started jogging behind Ms. Penrod. Lola joined me.

"You're so lucky," Lola said.

"No I'm not," I huffed. "I'm jogging."

"Yeah, but when the rest of us are stuck doing cruddy sit-ups, you get to practice bear moves all by yourself while the boys watch you."

"Huh?" I asked. I didn't know the boys watched me. Why hadn't Lola mentioned this to me before?

"Yeah. They stand underneath the bleachers and watch you practice."

I didn't want that happening. I wasn't ready to be seen yet. That was why it was called practice.

"Four more laps!" Ms. Penrod said.

"I can't wait to see how things go with Jasper and Annabelle," Lola said.

"I know," I huffed. "They could be talking right now." But I wasn't really thinking about Annabelle. I was thinking about the boys watching me.

"Are you going to work on your growling today?" Lola asked.

I was a little bit surprised to hear this question because I hadn't been aware that Lola watched me when I practiced growling. I'd thought everybody was exercising while I was off to the side doing my own thing. I'd had no idea so many eyeballs were on me. It made me feel self-conscious.

"I think I'm just going to stretch and practice silent growling," I said.

"Bears stretch?" Lola asked. "How boring."

I didn't like to think I was boring. But I just kept jogging.

"Don't forget to breathe!" Ms. Penrod hollered at us.

But I was breathing quite a bit. And sweating. Bleh.

Once we finished jogging, we gathered in a circle around Ms. Penrod. A couple of girls flopped down on the floor, but Ms. Penrod did not enjoy seeing this.

"Get back up and keep moving. Walk in place," she firmly instructed. "You want to stay warmed up."

Walk. Walk. Walk. While I walked, my mind drifted to Sylvie. She didn't have to take PE at her school. She took dance. I bet she didn't have to warm up for her dance class by doing sweaty jogging and boring stretching.

"Your abdominals are the core of your body," Ms. Penrod said.

We kept moving.

"They support your entire framework. They are made up of six muscles. And in addition to supporting your trunk, they hold your internal organs in place."

I did not enjoy thinking about my internal organs.

"Your six abdominal muscles have names: transverse abdominis, rectus abdominis, a pair of external obliques, and a pair of internal obliques."

"I bet we have a quiz on this," Lola said.

But I didn't say anything back. Because when Ms. Penrod talked, all I did was listen.

"We will identify where these muscles are located and then we will alternate between crunches and curls to strengthen them," Ms. Penrod said. "Ready, campers?"

I don't know why she liked calling us campers, but she did. We all got down on the floor and waited for more instructions. But I didn't get any. I got a tap on the shoulder. And it was Ms. Penrod tapping me.

"I know mascot clinic didn't turn out the way you'd hoped," she said.

"No, it really didn't," I said.

"I've brought in a special trainer for you today," Ms. Penrod said. And then she squeezed my shoulder in a happy way.

I blinked at her. Because I hadn't expected Ms. Penrod to be this helpful.

"Hi, Bessica!" a person with red hair said to me.

"Hi," I said, waving a little bit.

"It's me! Vicki Docker! I cut my hair."

Ooh! I waved more enthusiastically. I'd met Vicki and her twin sister, Marci, a few weeks before I started middle school. Even though they were in high school, my mom had invited them over for pizza so they could tell me what to expect when I started middle school. And they gave me lots of great advice. Like don't stand in front of Dolan the Puker in chorus and avoid the Crispito at lunch.

"Vicki was a stellar mascot," Ms. Penrod said. "And I think she'll help fill in the blanks for you."

Before my school split into North and South, Vicki was the Teton Middle School Bee. And while I wasn't sure exactly what an ex-bee could teach me, a bear, I was hopeful I'd learn something. Because my game was coming up and I knew almost zero about how to be an awesome mascot. I smiled at Vicki. Ms. Penrod still hadn't left yet.

"She possesses unmatched vigor, and I think she can teach you how to be a champion bear," Ms. Penrod said.

"Okay," I said.

"So cool!" Vicki said. "Let's get started!"

And I thought it was pretty cool that I didn't have to learn how to exercise my six stomach muscles. We walked to the other side of the gym. And for the first time I noticed some of the boys hanging out behind the bleachers watching me.

"Do the gawkers bother you?" Vicki asked, pointing to the boys.

"A little bit," I said.

She pointed her finger at me in a very excited way. "It shouldn't! Because you have the skills required to work an audience!"

"I do?" I asked.

"Bessica," she said, putting a hand on my shoulder. "From the moment I met you I could see your inner cheer beast trying to break free."

I didn't know I had an inner cheer beast stuck inside me.

"You can't care what anybody else thinks. You've got to follow your beast instincts or you'll never be authentic." Vicki spoke in a way that sounded very serious.

And just then Ms. Penrod showed up and stood next to Vicki.

"I'm teaching her about being authentic," Vicki explained to Ms. Penrod.

Then I felt Ms. Penrod touch me on the shoulder, and she held me with her pawlike hands for several seconds while she looked deep into my eyes. "Being authentic means that you're brave enough to represent your mascot animal in a sincere way. You're not playing around."

"Right," Vicki added. "It means that you commit yourself to acting like a bear to the point where you actually develop a bear's personality."

"Oh," I said. That made a ton of sense. Because a mascot bear would have the personality of a bear. I thought that was what Duke and Pierre had been trying to tell me but with different words.

"That's what made me such a successful bee," Vicki explained. "I read about bees. I watched movies about bees.

I even went out and got stung a couple of times so I could fully understand the power of the stinger."

"Wow," I said.

"She was a phenomenal bee," Ms. Penrod said. "Vicki went all the way to nationals."

Vicki blushed. "And I almost won the whole shebang."

I'd never heard of a shebang before, but Vicki still seemed pretty sad that she'd lost it.

"My dad wants to take me to Bear Galaxy," I said.

Vicki's and Ms. Penrod's faces lit up.

"That's great!" Vicki said.

"Yes. That's fantastic! I love to see parental support," Ms. Penrod said. "I'm going to let Vicki lead you through a few cheers. I've got stomachs to shape up."

I watched Ms. Penrod walk off. It made me happy to think that she cared so much about my performance level.

"First things first," Vicki said. "You need to come up with your basic five head-on cheers and your basic five head-off cheers."

I nodded. Because this was about the only thing I'd learned at mascot clinic before I got caged in the cafeteria.

"Okay," Vicki said. "Here's the deal. In some mascot circles it's taboo to take the head off in public," Vicki said. "But you're a sixth grader. So you should take the head off whenever it feels heavy or you feel deprived of fresh air."

"Uh-huh," I said. But then I had a question that I can't believe I hadn't already asked Duke or Pierre. *What would I do with my bear head once I took it off?* It was as if Vicki could read my mind.

"Whenever you take off your bear head, make sure you set it on a chair and not the ground," Vicki said.

"Because somebody might accidentally kick it?" I asked.

Vicki looked surprised by that concern. "No. It's bad luck to put your head on the floor."

"Right," I said.

"Moving on. Some cheers can easily be performed while wearing your head," she said. "But others require the head to be taken off."

"Makes sense," I said. Vicki was a mascot genius.

"So how many cheers do you know?" Vicki asked.

"Two!" I said excitedly.

As soon as I'd realized at mascot clinic that everybody else knew cheers, I'd gone online and searched for some good ones.

"Let 'em rip," Vicki said.

And I did. I clapped and swung my arms around and started. "Let's push back. DEFENSE! Push 'em back. DE-FENSE! Sack that quarterback! Grr!"

Vicki didn't smile as much as I hoped she would when I finished. "What's your other cheer?"

"Hey! Bears! SCORE! Hey! Bears! Win!" Then I clapped. "I say score! I say win! Go, Bears! *Grrr*."

Vicki folded her arms across her chest. "Do you feel like a bear when you yell these things?"

I shook my head. Because I mostly felt like myself when I yelled these things. Except the part where I growled.

"I could growl for much longer," I said.

"Yeah, that's not enough," Vicki said.

And I totally believed her.

"Okay. I'm going to focus on head-off cheers with you today. There are things you need to know."

"Cool," I said. I was hot from jogging, and even though I loved wearing the costume, I didn't feel like practicing with the head on at the moment.

"First, I need to be honest with you," Vicki said. "Your cheers are weak."

"They are?" I asked. Because I'd found them on the Internet when I searched for *popular cheers*.

"They aren't bear authentic. And they don't talk enough smack."

"I'm supposed to be a bear who talks smack?" I asked. Nobody had mentioned that to me yet.

"That's really the whole point of being a mascot. You talk smack to the other team, but mainly the opposing team's mascot."

"Oh," I said.

"You say things that make it look like you're going to fight each other."

"I do?" I asked. I was unsure how I felt about that. I'd never said fighting words before.

"Yeah," Vicki said. "It's all part of why people watch you."

Then Vicki taught me how to stand in ways that reflected my bearness.

"This is one stance I used to use for the bee," Vicki said, sticking her butt out really far. "And this is how we should modify it for a bear."

She squatted down a little.

"Doesn't this look more like a bear to you?" she asked.

"No," I said. Then I thought of an important question, so I asked it. "Why aren't you in high school right now?"

"It was a half day, and Ms. Penrod wanted me to come and help catch you up to speed. She said you'd missed the mascot clinic. And I'm glad I came. We need to dial up your bear mojo."

"What's mojo?" I asked.

"It's the magic quality that all good, charismatic mascots have."

"How do I dial it up?" I asked.

Vicki backed away from me and clapped her hands

together. "Okay. If you ever feel your mojo waning, you should have a couple of comic go-to moves."

Things felt very advanced. It was like Vicki thought she was talking to a high school person and not a sixth grader.

"Here's one of my favorite comic moves." Vicki swung her arms in circles. "Windmill arms!" *Faster. Faster.* "It's funny because it's a countermove. Audiences like it because it's an action that runs counter to an animal's natural behavior."

It did look funny.

"Jumping rope is a good mojo-building countermove for you," Vicki said. "Got it?"

At the mention of "mojo-building countermove," Alice Potgeiser came bouncing into the room. "Vicki!" she cheered.

They knew each other because when Vicki was the bee, Alice was a cheerleader. And so they'd cheered at lots of games together. I was surprised that Vicki liked Alice. Because Vicki seemed like such a decent person. And Alice Potgeiser seemed like a jerkwad.

But maybe Vicki liked jerkwads. Because Alice ran full speed toward her and Vicki stopped making windmill arms and they hugged each other. It made me gag a little. Then they stopped hugging and Alice asked, "Why are you here?"

"I'm teaching Bessica some cheers," Vicki said.

Alice did not enjoy hearing this. Her lip curled into a snarl. "You are?"

And it was like I could read Alice Potgeiser's mind. She was upset that Vicki was teaching me cheers because Alice was hoping I wouldn't learn any good cheers and would show up and suck. It felt terrible to know that the person I shared mascot duties with wanted me to look terrible in front of the entire school. I was beginning to think she *had* locked me in Flat Creek's cafeteria during mascot clinic.

"Bessica is cheering against T.J. the Snake River Tiger," Alice said.

Vicki looked at me and her eyes got huge. "You're so brave!"

"No I'm not," I said. Because it wasn't like I was going to be cheering against a real tiger. It was just a boy named T.J. in a mascot costume with an excellent swishy tail.

"T.J. talks more smack than anybody. And he has a crazy-loud cheer voice," Vicki said.

"Super-crazy-loud," Alice added. "And sometimes he plays pranks."

"Huh," I said. Alice and Vicki were freaking me out a little bit.

"Yeah, he's a prankster," Vicki said. "You can't turn your back on him. He likes to stick signs on mascots."

"What kind of signs?" I asked.

"Rude signs," Vicki said. "It's part of his shtick."

The things coming out of Vicki's mouth were starting to make me feel nervous.

"Don't make that face," Vicki said. "Everything is going to be fine. You'll love being mascot. Just learn five good cheers to chant with the bear head on, and five good cheers to chant with the bear head off, and never turn your back on T.J. the Tiger."

"That's a lot to remember," I said.

"But you're a natural," Vicki said. "Here."

Then she handed me a piece of paper with a bunch of cheers written on the front and back.

"They're seven of the best cheers I know," Vicki said.

I glanced through them. They were all bear cheers. "This is really nice of you," I said.

"Knock 'em dead!" Vicki said.

Then she and Alice walked off giggling. And I took my cheer sheet and started trying to memorize all the cheers. Some of them seemed a little mean, but I learned them anyway. Because if Vicki Docker told me it was important to talk smack, then I was going to do just that.

CHAPTER

"**I** can't believe you want to feed a lizard," my mom said as Noll was carrying the aquarium from our front door into my bedroom.

When I'd learned that Noll would be relocating his lizard to my bedroom and that I wouldn't be venturing over to his bedroom to feed Bianca, the arrangement had become a little less exciting. But I didn't admit that to anybody.

"It will be great," I said.

"Do the crickets ever escape?" my mom asked. Her face was very wrinkled with concern.

Noll had been extra conscientious and brought us a bag of crickets that he'd already gut loaded with vitamins. He was going to give us a quick lesson on how to feed Bianca.

"The top is a little loose, so on occasion they do escape," Noll said as he set the aquarium down right next to my jewelry box. "But if you coat them in the calcium powder I brought they turn a bright white color and are very easy to spot on carpet."

My mom and I looked down at my green bedroom carpet. It suddenly seemed obvious that we were going to have to capture escaped crickets.

"Add roughly a tablespoon of the calcium powder," Noll said.

I watched Noll open the plastic bag, drop in the powder, and shake it ferociously. The little crickets inside were smaller than dimes and they bounced around inside the plastic until they were ghost white.

"Now you dump them in the cage." Noll lifted the corner of the lid off, tipped the bag, and poured the white crickets into the aquarium. Bianca must have been starving. Because she raced over to a group of them and snapped up three very quickly.

"Whoa," I said.

"When will you be back?" my mom asked.

"Two weeks," Noll said.

"But your parents will be collecting Bianca and her setup before then, right?" my mom asked.

"Or we can keep Bianca here until you get back," I said. "I don't mind."

I glanced at my mom and smiled. But she didn't smile back.

"You're so awesome, Bessica," Noll said.

"I know," I said.

"You've got my cell number, right?" he asked.

"I do," I said. My life felt pretty wonderful.

"Call if you need anything," he said.

"I will," I said. This was one of the best conversations I'd ever had in my whole life.

I walked him to the door and then watched gorgeous Noll Beck leave my house. I stared through the window as he walked back across our yard.

"Aah!" my mom screamed. It was coming from my bedroom, so I ran there.

Wow. The top must have been a little loose, like Noll said. Because on the carpet I spotted three white crickets racing under my bed.

"Gross," I said.

"Do you think your grandma is going to enjoy living in a house with crickets and a lizard?"

I smiled huge when my mom said this. Because Grandma was coming home today!

"Mom," I said. "Grandma is going to be so excited to see us that she probably won't notice the crickets or Bianca for a week."

My mother rolled her eyes. "Are you going to pick them up?"

"They're already under my bed," I said.

"You're just going to let them live under there?" my mom asked.

My dad walked into my room. "Why the scream?" Then he looked at the lizard cage. "I always wanted a lizard. Noll Beck is a lucky young man."

"I don't feel lucky," my mom said.

Then I heard something that sounded like a car in the driveway. "Maybe that's Grandma!" So I grabbed the sign I'd made using markers, glitter, and ribbons that said DON'T EVER LEAVE AGAIN, GRANDMA and ran as fast as I could.

But it wasn't her.

Waiting in the front yard for Grandma to show up while holding my sign was one of the most exciting things I'd ever done in my whole life. I hadn't seen Grandma in over six weeks. And any minute she was going to be back home. I didn't realize one person could miss another person as much as I'd missed Grandma. It sort of made the fact that Sylvie hated me and had uninvited me from her birthday party matter a little less.

While I stood by the mailbox and stared at the road and waited and waited and waited, I wondered what fun things Grandma and I would do once she got back. We'd go to the mall. We'd go to the park. And she'd start making me desserts again!

"You could wait inside," my mom said.

I jumped a little. I hadn't even known my mom was standing by me and the mailbox.

"I want to see her as soon as she gets here," I said.

"Maybe you should do something besides wait," my mom said.

That was a pretty good suggestion. I set my sign on the grass and placed a small rock on it and pulled out my phone. "I'll text Grandma."

Me: How much longer until you are here?

"They might be out of range," my mother explained.

But they weren't, because my phone buzzed. And it was a message from Grandma.

Grandma: About an hour away! See you soon!

"She's an hour away," I said.

"Looks like you've got time to do something productive."

"I am not doing homework right now," I said. Ever since I started middle school, my mom had started frequently reminding me that I always had homework. Bleh.

"Not homework," my mom said. "But maybe you could practice your mascot routine."

"That's a great idea," I said. "Because I perform against the tiger in a week."

My mother looked at me in a disapproving way. And I had no idea why.

"What?" I asked.

"You're not performing *against* the tiger," my mom said. "You're performing *for* your school."

I shook my head. Wow. I had never realized this about my mom before, but she didn't understand basic mascot rules. "Actually," I said, "I'm totally competing with the tiger. In fact, the crowd loves it when the mascots fight."

"Who told you that?"

"Vicki Docker."

My mom smiled. "You're still in touch with the Docker twins?"

I nodded. But I didn't bother telling my mom that Vicki had come to my PE class to coach me. Because my mom would have wanted all the details. And there were a lot of those, and that would have taken too much time to explain.

"I should probably put my bear paws on and practice in the grass," I said.

"You'll stain them," my mom said. "Why don't you practice inside?"

But the more I thought about it, the more sense it made to practice acting like a bear outside in the wilderness.

"Grass is better," I said. "It's bear authentic." I hurried to my room, waved to Bianca, and grabbed my bear paws. But I also thought about how mushy the grass felt on the way inside, so I also grabbed something to protect the fur: gigantic plastic trash bags. I sat on the sidewalk and started tucking the plastic around my paws.

"What are you doing?" my dad asked.

I looked up at him. He was holding his laser jammer.

"What are *you* doing?" I asked. Because I thought the laser jammer belonged in the car.

"Registering my unit," he explained.

"Oh," I said. I didn't like that he was registering an illegal unit. "I'm wrapping my bear paws in plastic so they don't get grass stains on them."

"Are you going to be able to jump rope like that?" he asked.

"Probably," I said. Jumping rope was my special talent that won me my mascot position. I wasn't going to give that up.

I finished tucking the plastic in all the way around my bear paws so it went in the hole for my foot. I heard the front door open behind me.

"There's no way that will work, Bessica," my mom said. "You're going to slip and hurt yourself."

I didn't know why both my parents had decided to be so negative. "It's fine," I said. "I'm going to practice my bear stances."

I was so lucky Vicki had come and offered me such fantastic ideas.

"Roar!" I said, swinging my arms out wide. "Score!" I yelled. Then I swung my arms very quickly, yelling, *"Roar!* Score! *Roar!* Score!"

When I looked at my parents, they were both laughing at me.

"Nice bear stance," my dad said. Then he swung his own arms just like I had, and I didn't really appreciate that.

"Do you know another cheer?" my mom asked.

"Yes," I said. I'd taken Vicki's cheers and added a few of my own touches. I stood with my feet apart to give myself the best balance possible. "I want a touchdown! I want a trout! If you get in my way, I'll rip your guts out!" Then I fell to my knees and unleashed the biggest roar ever and clawed at the air in front of me.

My parents did not laugh at this. They looked a little stunned.

"You're going to threaten to rip the guts out of the opposing team's players?" my dad asked.

But I shook my head. That wasn't what my cheer meant at all. "No, Dad. I'm threatening the guts of the other mascot. They're going to yell similar things to me. It's called talking smack."

My parents looked at each other.

"And you're going to fall down on your knees like that on the football stadium turf?" my mom asked. "You'll stain your costume."

I looked down at the knee area of my grass-stained jeans and shook my head. "The costume is brown. You won't be able to see grass stains."

Then I decided to show them another cheer. "Imagine that I'm jumping rope," I said. I pretended to do that. "Roll it! Shake it! Beat it up and bake it! Honey and sugar, you're gonna lose. Honey and sugar, eat our boos!" And then my mom and dad were supposed to boo like maniacs, but they didn't, so I booed for them.

"Boo!" I yelled. "Boo!"

Then I went into the second part of the cheer, which required a burst of energy. I jumped. "Win!" *Jump.* "Win!" *Jump.* "Win!"

Then I decided to pick up my jump rope. I jumped as fast as I could. *Swing, jump. Swing, jump. Swing, jump.*

"Holy cow," my dad said. "If you hit anybody with that rope, you'll knock them out."

"Be careful, Bessica," my mother said, taking a few steps back.

"Boo!" I hollered. "Boo!"

"Honestly," my mom said. "Do your cheers have to be so unkind?"

I stopped jumping rope. "Yes," I said. "That's what people want."

My dad shook his head. "They want to be entertained. You don't have to jeer so much."

I wasn't sure what the word *jeer* meant. But I didn't let that stop me from disagreeing with him. "Jeering isn't necessarily a bad thing."

Honk! Honk! Honk!

I turned and looked to where the driveway met the road. "Grandma!" I cried.

I ran toward the motor home as it turned into our driveway. I could see Grandma's arm waving at me from the passenger window. I picked up my sign and stayed on the grass as Willy drove up to our garage and parked, because I didn't know how good a driver he was and it seemed he could accidentally hit me if I got too close.

"Bessica!" Grandma cheered as she climbed out of the motor home.

I ran to her as fast as I could while holding up my sign.

"It's so good to see you!" I said. I handed her the sign, threw my arms around her waist, and squeezed her. She felt safe and familiar and good.

"Good to see you, Willy," my dad said.

I turned my face toward my dad and glared at him a little. I didn't think we should be encouraging Willy. That was why I didn't put his name on the sign.

"Your pixie cut is getting so long," Grandma said.

"It is?" I asked as I reached up and touched it.

"It's getting to that point where you'll have to decide whether you want to let it turn into a bob. Or re-pixie it."

"Really?" I asked. I didn't know those were my two choices.

"Is Sylvie growing hers out too?" Grandma asked.

Seeing Grandma again *and* thinking about Sylvie at the exact same time made me sad.

"I think so," I said. I figured guessing was the best answer.

"What's on your feet?" Grandma asked. "Are they slippers?"

Then I got very excited, because Grandma had never seen my bear paws!

"They're my hind paws!" I said. "Check them out." I

tugged the plastic off them and slipped them off my feet and handed them to Grandma. She handed Willy the sign and took them.

"Nice!" she said.

"They look very ferocious," Willy added. Then he made a lame growling noise.

"These give me an idea," Grandma said.

"What?" I asked. Because I thought maybe she wanted to make her own set of hind paws so we could match, and that seemed like fun.

"We should all visit Bear Galaxy together," she said.

"I've already suggested that," Dad said.

"Are there real bears at Bear Galaxy?" Willy asked.

"Of course," I said. What a terrible question. Could Willy have been any more lame?

"Once, in Alaska, I came toe to toe with a polar bear," Willy said.

That was actually pretty cool. "Did you shoot it?" I asked. Because Mr. Hoser had told us that polar bears were the most vicious bears that had ever walked on Earth.

"I did not," Willy said, taking one of my paws in his hands.

"Did a person you were with shoot it?" I asked. Based on what Mr. Hoser had told us, I was pretty sure the only way to escape a polar bear was by killing it.

"The person I was with shot it with bear spray and we took off on a snowmobile," Willy said, crossing his heart with his index finger. "True tale."

"Wow," my dad said. "Great story."

But I didn't think it was great. I thought it was just okay.

"Let's fix some snacks," Grandma said.

"Do you need me to help you carry your things inside?" I asked.

Grandma shook her head. "Willy and I are staying in the Winnebago."

"Huh?" I asked. Why would Grandma want to stay inside that awful thing when she could come inside the house and live with us again? This was all so confusing.

"Bessica!" Willy called. I turned back around and looked at him.

"What?" I asked.

"I brought you something," he said.

I wanted to roll my eyes, but I stopped myself from doing that. Didn't Willy understand that he bothered me?

"Here," Willy said.

He handed me a key chain with a bear on it.

"It's a grizzly bear," he said. "Like you."

I felt like telling Willy that I was a mascot, not a grizzly bear. I stuck the key chain in my pocket without even looking at it very closely.

"Thanks," I said.

"We got something for Sylvie too," Grandma said. "Isn't her birthday coming up?"

I didn't even answer.

"Yes," my mom said. "Bessica bought her a surprise present. She isn't telling anybody what it is."

"Ooh," Grandma said. "I bet she tells me."

Was this the right time to tell Grandma that due to a war of texts, Sylvie had uninvited me to her party and that we were no longer friends? No.

"I want it to stay a surprise," I said.

I thought back to what I'd bought Sylvie at the mall that day. Thinking about it now, what I got might be seen as a little bit of a mean gift. I had looked up her nose and seen all that hair. And I'd spotted a battery-powered nose hair trimmer and thought that would be perfect. So I'd bought it and wrapped it and stuffed it under my bed. But it didn't matter much now. Because how could you go to a disco/jungle–theme birthday party when you weren't even talking to the person who was throwing it?

CHAPTER

10

Something had happened to Annabelle. She hated me. One day we were fine and I was giving her fantastic advice about Jasper. The next day she wouldn't even talk to me. At first I thought maybe I was imagining that Annabelle was giving me the silent treatment. But then Lola tracked me down before lunch.

"Annabelle is furious with you and has asked that you not eat lunch with us anymore." Lola seemed bummed when she told me this.

"Why?" I asked. I thought I'd been a pretty good friend to Annabelle. What had I done? Why was she mad at me? Who would I eat lunch with? This was all terrible news.

"It's about Jasper," Lola said.

"Oh yeah," I said. "I forgot about that. How did it go?"

Lola bit her bottom lip. "I don't think I should tell you. I think she should tell you."

"But she doesn't even want to talk to me," I argued.

Lola took a big breath and held it. She studied my face before she released it. "Her talk with Jasper was a disaster."

"What happened?" I asked.

Lola huffed a little. "I already said I think Annabelle should be the one to tell you, not me."

"Right," I said. "Hey, maybe I could write Annabelle an apology really quickly and you could give it to her and maybe we could forgive each other and eat lunch together."

I was impressed I could think on my feet so quickly.

"That's pretty doubtful," Lola said. "She's so upset I'm surprised she even came to school."

I tore a piece of paper from my binder and tried to write the apology I'd want if I were Annabelle.

> Hi, Annabelle. I am SO SO SO sorry to hear about Jasper. You are AWESOME and he doesn't deserve your kindness or attention. PLEASE don't be mad at ME. I was only trying to help. Let's talk.
> FEEL BETTER! BL

"Will you read this and tell me what you think?" I asked Lola.

Her eyes darted left to right and back as she read it. "It looks pretty good. Wait here and I'll be right back."

"Okay," I said. "But if I'm not here, I'll be by the vending machine buying my lunch." I didn't like to buy a zero-nutrition lunch from the vending machine, but it was better than eating alone in the cafeteria wishing I were eating with my friends. Or starving all by myself.

Lola hurried off with my note and I hung out by my locker until I heard footsteps. *Squeak. Squeak. Squeak.* Uh-oh. They belonged to my middle school's hall monitor, Cameron Bon Qui Qui. She was incredibly hung up on rules, and I found her to be a mean drag of a human being.

"I'm not doing anything wrong," I told her as I stood by my locker. Because she loved calling me a hallway violator.

"I have eyes," Cameron Bon Qui Qui said. "I can see that you're behaving yourself."

And then she didn't say anything else and we just stood there looking at each other. I thought maybe she wanted to tell me something.

"What?" I finally asked.

Cameron Bon Qui Qui looked left and right. Then she took a step toward me and she stood so close I could feel her breath touch my face. "This is no joke. I'm here to warn you."

When she said this I looked left and right too.

"You're in danger. The game. This Friday. T.J. has something planned." Cameron Bon Qui Qui spoke very quickly and didn't give me any time to respond. "He's working on a new trick. Something that can cause substantial bodily harm. It's called a facebomb, and—"

"Hey," I said, cutting her off. "You're freaking me out."

Cameron Bon Qui Qui nodded. "You should be freaked out! You're running a serious risk of permanent injury and/or humiliation. And think of our school. You're our mascot. You represent all of us. Letting T.J. facebomb you would be like letting T.J. facebomb every student at North Teton Middle School. You can't let that happen." She took a step back and looked at the wall clock. "I'm late for a hall monitor meeting. Enjoy lunch."

Squeak. Squeak. Squeak.

Cameron Bon Qui Qui left faster than she'd arrived. I hardly had a chance to catch my breath before Lola came racing up.

"Pronto! Pronto!" Lola said. "Get to the upstairs girls' bathroom."

"Is this an earthquake drill?" I asked.

"No. Annabelle wants to talk to you alone in the second stall."

"Oh," I said.

"Go!" Lola said, giving me a shove.

I moved very fast because Lola had made this bathroom meeting feel like the most urgent thing ever. I pushed open the wood door and immediately started looking under the stalls at people's shoes. All the stalls were empty. Then I heard the door open and I turned around and it was Annabelle. She looked furious!

"Hi," I said, waving. "How are you?"

Annabelle didn't answer me. She just walked to the second bathroom stall. She pointed her finger at me and then at the toilet. Which I assumed meant that she wanted me to join her in the stall. So I did. Once the door was shut I wasn't sure who should start talking first, so I went.

"How did things go with Jasper?" I asked.

Annabelle narrowed her bright eyes and held back tears. "He thinks I'm a crazy dweeb."

"No," I said. "There's no way. Why do you think Jasper thinks that?"

Annabelle pulled her phone out of her pocket and turned it on. I didn't bother telling her that phones weren't allowed in school, because I sneaked mine to school too. Annabelle scrolled down through her text messages. There were a lot from Jasper.

"Wow!" I said. "You two really hit it off."

Annabelle scowled at me. "Read this," she said, shoving her phone in my face.

Jasper: You are a crazy dweeb.

It was shocking to see that Jasper had texted Annabelle such a rude message.

"What a creep!" I said.

Annabelle closed the message. "He is not! I still like him."

My mouth dropped open. "You can't," I said. "After somebody is a jerk like that, you have to get over them right away."

"Don't you understand?" Annabelle said. "I wanted Jasper to be my boyfriend."

Tears spilled down Annabelle's cheeks. This was going to be a much harder conversation than I'd thought.

"After he texted you that, did you text anything back?" I asked.

Annabelle sniffled. "I sent him a message that said, 'No, you're a crazy dweeb.'"

While that sounded reasonable under the circumstances, I was pretty sure that was *not* the best way to get Jasper to become her boyfriend.

"How did you two even start texting?" I asked. "You'd never even spoken to him until a couple of days ago."

Annabelle sniffled more. "The conversation in English went really well in the beginning. But then things turned terrible."

When she said the word *terrible* she burst into uncontrollable tears. I really wished I'd remembered to call her and ask about the Jasper situation closer to when it had happened. Because I felt very confused getting things piece by piece.

"Did you see him today?" I asked.

"He's absent," Annabelle said. "He thinks I'm so crazy and dweeby he doesn't even want to come to school."

"Maybe he's just sick," I said. "He's been sick before."

"Maybe," she said.

"My grandma once told me that there are always two ways to take something: the good way and the bad way. Don't take Jasper's absence the bad way."

This seemed to make Annabelle feel a tiny bit better. "But what about his text?"

I didn't have a good answer for that one. So I decided to open up to her about my own texting mistakes. "Once, I got into a war of texts with my best friend."

"Sylvie?" Annabelle asked.

I didn't really want to admit who I'd been in the war of texts with, but I also didn't want to lie.

"Yes," I said. "Sylvie texted me something that I didn't like. So I texted her something mean. Back and forth.

Back and forth. Until I texted Sylvie that she had ugly ears."

Annabelle gasped.

"The mean texts kept getting meaner, and I basically let them ruin my friendship with Sylvie. So I know exactly how you feel."

Annabelle threw her arms around me and almost knocked me over. "That's exactly what happened with Jasper. Our mean texts got meaner. He texted something dumb about our English teacher, Mrs. Flako, and it really bothered me, so I texted him something dumb about his brother."

"Ooh," I said. "It's always a bad idea to text people rude things about their family members."

"It was a joke!" Annabelle said.

The buzzer rang. Lunch was over.

"One of the things I looked forward to most at school was seeing Jasper. Now I sort of never want to see him ever again," Annabelle said. "But I'm also sort of dying to see him."

That sounded very complicated. I was glad that wasn't how I felt about my gorgeous neighbor, Noll Beck.

"Should I start texting him apologies?" Annabelle asked me.

"Don't touch your phone," I urged.

"But I have to do something," Annabelle said. "I need closure."

"Just be nice to Jasper next time you see him," I said. "There's got to be a way to fix this situation."

I didn't necessarily believe that. But I wanted to improve Annabelle's mood.

"What are you going to do to fix things with Sylvie?" Annabelle asked.

Sylvie. Why did friendship have to be so hard? How could sending a bunch of texts end this badly?

"I'm going to wait things out," I said.

"How long will that take?" Annabelle asked.

"I have no idea."

CHAPTER

11

I hated thinking about T.J. the Tiger and how he wanted to facebomb me. And I hated thinking about missing Sylvie's disco/jungle party. But more than anything, I hated Willy's Winnebago and how it sat in our driveway with Grandma inside it.

"How are five people going to fit in your car?" I asked my mom. "It's going to be uncomfortable." I wasn't sure how long it would take to get to Bear Galaxy.

"There will be six people," my mom said.

"What?" I asked. Then I wondered if maybe we were taking the Winnebago. Which seemed dangerous. Because a bear would attack anything with food inside it and Willy's Winnebago had a refrigerator.

"Our friend Alma is coming and we're taking two cars," my mom said.

"When did Alma become our friend?" I asked. Because the last lady who worked at the podiatrist's office had never become our friend. She filed everything wrong and made my mom's life harder. And until she got let go we all complained about her a lot.

"She's been wanting to go to Bear Galaxy since she moved to the area," my mom explained. "She doesn't know a lot of people yet."

"Okay," I mumbled.

"So have you decided which car you're riding in?" my dad asked.

I hadn't. Because the whole Alma thing had just been sprung on me.

"I'll go with Grandma," I said. Because I really wanted to see bears with her.

"Okay," my dad said. "Looks like they've got a full car."

That was when I did some math in my head and realized that four people would be traveling in Alma's car and two of them would be people I didn't really like all that well: Willy and Alma.

"I don't want Willy in our car," I said.

"Shhh," my mom said. "Don't say that." Then she did some looking around to make sure nobody had heard me.

"You can't boot Willy," my dad said. "He and Grandma are a couple."

"Right," I said.

"You'll have a lot of fun in that car," my mom said. "Alma used to work in a veterinarian's office. She knows a lot about animals."

Knock. Knock. Knock.

And then I couldn't believe it. Alma didn't wait for us to answer the door. She walked right into our house.

"Ready to roll?" Alma asked. She was wearing jeans and a red jacket that looked like it was made out of plastic.

"We've figured out seating arrangements," my dad said. "Looks like Bessica will be traveling with you."

"Wonderful!" Alma said.

"Hold the phone," I said. Then I ran to my mom's side and so I wouldn't hurt anybody's feelings, whispered my new preference. "I think I want to travel with you and dad. And I want to roll the window down just enough that I can stick my phone outside and take bear pictures."

My mother sighed and whispered back, "You can ride along with me and your dad, but you can't roll down the windows. It's against park rules."

And then we all buckled up and headed off.

As we drove to Bear Galaxy my parents had a very boring discussion about the laser jammer.

"I can't believe you brought it," my mom said.

"But I don't even have it plugged in," my dad said.

"It's illegal," my mom said.

"Technically, radar scramblers are illegal. And radar jammers are illegal. But laser jammers are still okay in every state except Minnesota."

I couldn't take it anymore. "Boring!" I called from the backseat.

My mother turned around and looked at me. "And what would you like to talk about?" she asked.

I sat straight up and tucked a piece of my hair behind my ear. "I want to know how many bears you think we'll see today."

My dad laughed. "Black bears or grizzly bears, or do you want me to group them together?"

"Group them together," I said. Because I loved big numbers.

"I bet we see seventy bears," my dad said.

My heart was beating very fast. "Holy crud! I was thinking we'd see twenty."

"They've got a lot," my mom said. "Plus all the cubs."

My stomach flipped. I'd forgotten about the cubs.

"Plus we'll see some wolves," my dad said.

"I love wolves!" I said. Even though I'd never seen one

before. Because last time we went to Bear Galaxy they didn't have the wolves yet.

"Look!" my mom said. "We're here."

I stared at the big wooden gates for Bear Galaxy. The road leading to the entrance was pure dirt, and a cloud rose around our car as we drove.

"Is Grandma still behind us?" I asked, twisting around to look out the back window.

Through the dirt puff I could see Alma's car. All three of them were sitting in the front seat. Yuck. I'd hoped Willy would sit in the back. I waved to Grandma while my dad rolled down the window and paid the entrance fee.

"Do you have any food in the car that might attract the bears?" the man asked.

"No," my father said.

"Okay," the man said. "Here's a pamphlet to familiarize yourself with Bear Galaxy and our rules."

"Thanks!" I yelled from the backseat. I did not want this guy to tell us more about Bear Galaxy. I wanted to drive through the gates and experience it.

"Enjoy your adventure," the man said.

"Okay!" I yelled.

Driving through the gates was very thrilling. They were the tallest gates I'd ever driven through in my life. The wood posts went up nearly as high as telephone poles.

"This is awesome!" I said.

My dad drove very slowly as we approached wires in the road. There was a big yellow sign that said we should not straddle the wires or we could risk electrocution.

"Why do we have to drive over these wires?" I asked. It seemed very dangerous.

"The first section of the park is where they keep the grizzly bears. They have to electrify the perimeter or they could escape or attack the cars."

"What?" I said. It was scary to think that a bear might attack our car.

"These bears are dangerous, so they're kept behind the electric fence," my mom explained. "Once we get to the black bear section there won't be any electric fences. Black bears aren't as dangerous."

"Oh," I said. "So a black bear has never killed a person?"

"It's rare," my dad said.

"So a black bear *has* killed a person?" I asked.

"Let's not talk about this," my mom said. "Let's watch the grizzly bears."

That was a good suggestion, because there were dozens of grizzly bears sleeping in the grass.

"Oh my heck!" I said. "They're everywhere!"

My dad slowly followed the car in front of us as we rounded corners and saw fluffy brown bear after fluffy brown bear.

"They don't look ferocious," I said. "They look zonked."

"They can flip into attack mode on a dime." My dad gripped the steering wheel. "Never trust a bear."

Then our car approached another set of wires.

"We're leaving the grizzly bear area," my dad said.

"Really?" I asked. Because that seemed to go by pretty fast. "Can you drive slower?"

"Sure thing," he said. "Time to cross over the wires again."

"Would we really get electrocuted if we straddled them wrong?" I asked.

"Yep," my dad said.

"That's terrible!" I said. "I can't believe they electrocute bears here." Because I was a mascot bear and had recently been locked in a cafeteria, I began to feel very sympathetic toward my fellow creatures.

"Relax," my dad said in a calm voice. "They only shock the ones trying to escape."

"That's cruel!" I said. "Because how is a bear supposed to know that it's not allowed freedom?"

Seeing all these bears stripped of their right to be bears made me think a lot about my own bear duties at games. When I cheered against the tiger, I needed to show all the fans that bears were ferocious beasts that deserved to live in the wilderness and be as terrible as they wanted to be.

"What are you thinking about?" my mom asked me.

"My duties," I said.

I watched all the bears sleeping by the side of the road.

"Isn't this exciting?" my mother asked.

I shrugged.

"They're so big that moving around must make them tired," my mother said.

I frowned at this. "I know a lot about bears and I don't think that's true. They're bored. And depressed. How do these bears even get here? Do they capture them from Yellowstone?"

"No, no, no," my father said. "They don't capture them. Most of them are born here. Look at that one. It's walking around like a crazy, wild bear."

I watched a black bear mope in front of our car and sit down.

"Don't hit it!" I said.

"I'm not going to," my dad said.

But our car was still moving a little bit.

"Stop!" I said.

So he did.

"I think you're supposed to nudge it to get it to move," he said.

"That's a terrible idea," I said. Because that was basically almost running over a bear, and I knew we weren't allowed to do that. Even though we'd paid a bunch of money to visit the preserve.

"We're supposed to honk our horn," my mom said.

So my dad blared the horn. But the bear didn't even look at our car. The beast stood looking at its paw. And licking it.

"Don't honk at it!" I said.

I couldn't believe that my dad didn't have any respect for bears.

"I'm supposed to," my dad said. "This bear is causing a traffic jam."

I looked behind us. There were a lot of cars stopped in a line. Things were pretty backed up. I could see Grandma and Willy and Alma in the car behind us. They were chatting and looked thrilled. Apparently, they didn't understand that we were experiencing a bear-jam situation.

My dad honked again. This time for longer. That was when I started freaking out and reading the information packet.

"Stop with the long honks!" I said. "You're supposed to give your horn three quick beeps!"

"A bear can understand that?" my father asked, sounding impressed. "Wow."

So my father tapped on the horn, and within seconds a preserve ranger came running out toward the bear.

"Is he going to shoot the bear with a tranquilizer and

drag it away?" I asked. Because I'd seen that happen on a nature show once and it was very dramatic.

"Maybe," my dad said.

"No," my mom said. "He's brought a tub of food."

I watched as the man waved the small yellow tub at the bear.

"Come here, Regina!" the man yelled.

"That bear's name is Regina!" I said. I loved that the black bear causing the traffic jam was a girl bear.

Regina rolled over onto all four of her legs. But she didn't leave the road.

"Do you think I should honk again?" my dad asked.

"No!" I said.

"I agree," my mom said. "I think the ranger has things under control."

The man held the food container up in the air and shook it a little.

"What do you think is in there?" I asked. I pictured all sorts of terrible things, like fish guts and intestines and raw kidneys.

The ranger took some of the food and threw it on the ground in front of him.

"Looks like dog food," my dad said.

This was crazy! It did look like dog food! The bear slowly moved off the road and started eating the pellets. I was disgusted. Because in addition to taking away all the bears' freedom and allowing them to get honked at by cars, Bear Galaxy was feeding them dog food. It seemed like this place should be illegal.

"Isn't a bear's natural diet fish and berries and tubers and nuts and mountain goats?" I asked.

I remembered reading that after I'd looked online for bear information after I became the mascot.

"I'm sure the bear's pellet food is a balanced blend of the nutrients that it needs to live in captivity," my mom said. "There are laws about this sort of thing."

I looked out the back window again to see if Willy and Grandma were watching the bear. And what I saw happening in their front seat disgusted me.

"They're kissing!" I screamed. "I don't want to see that."

"Then don't look," my mother said.

I turned around and stared into the front seat. My dad glanced in the rearview mirror.

"I don't want you to look at them either," I said.

I really thought it was time that Grandma dumped Willy and started living full-time in the house again. Because living in a motor home in our driveway was lame.

I turned around and looked at Willy and shot him daggers. But it didn't help. He and Grandma started kissing again.

"Make them stop!" I said. "It's gross."

"Bessica, Willy and Grandma are a couple. Deal with it," my mom said.

The car started moving again and I saw brand-new bears I hadn't seen before. I thought about what my mom had said. I hated to think of Grandma and Willy being a couple. Grandma deserved so much more.

"Half of all marriages end in divorce," I said.

I don't know why this statistic popped into my head, but it did. My mom whipped her head around with a face of total surprise.

"Have you been eavesdropping on their conversations?" she asked. "Do you know something?"

I felt terrible. Because this meant my mom thought it was possible that Willy and Grandma might get married. But I wasn't even thinking of anything that horrible. I was just focusing on how many couples get divorced every year.

"Let's mind our own business," my dad said.

"Okay," I said. But really, that wasn't how I felt on the inside. On the inside, I was thinking there must be a way to break up Grandma and Willy before they decided to do something as stupid as get married.

"Ooh," my mother squealed. "There's a pair of arctic wolves!"

I looked at them, but I wasn't very excited.

"It says here that they're a couple," my mom said.

"Wonderful," I said. But I thought it was obvious that they were a couple. Because they were the only two arctic wolves in the preserve. Then it hit me: just like the female arctic wolf who only had one choice of a mate, Grandma was limited to terrible Willy. I looked back at them. I knew what this problem needed. More arctic wolves. Lots and lots and lots of wolves.

CHAPTER

On the morning of Sylvie's birthday party I got out her present and sat on my floor and looked at the purple paper and admired what a good job I'd done wrapping the box. I felt terrible that I was going to miss her disco/jungle party. And I'd miss the chance to hang out with Raya Papas too. I regretted sending a lot of those texts.

Knock. Knock. Knock.

"I'm busy," I called from my bed. But that wasn't true. I just didn't feel like talking to anybody.

"It's your grandma!" a voice called through the door.

"Hi, Grandma," I said. "You can come in."

Because even though I was in a terrible mood, I still wanted to see Grandma.

She swung my door open and practically jumped into my room. "Are you looking forward to the party?" she asked. "Mrs. Potaski always makes the most amazing cakes."

"Yeah," I said. I didn't really feel like telling Grandma about how Sylvie had told my principal I had fungal foot and this somehow had led to rude text messages and how I eventually got uninvited to her birthday party. And how the present on my bed for Sylvie was a battery-powered nose hair trimmer.

"Do you know what I'm thinking?" Grandma asked me.

I looked up at her. She was smiling. I had no idea what she was thinking. "I think I should take you to the party! It would be great to see the Potaskis. Plus, I have to give Sylvie that present I bought her in Minnesota."

"Is it a bear key chain with a terrible paint job?"

And as soon as I said that I felt bad about criticizing my gift. But the paint *was* chipped, and also sort of sloppy. Instead of having defined teeth, my grizzly bear just had a pure white mouth. It didn't even have a tongue.

"You don't like your key chain? I thought it was a very appropriate gift," Grandma said. She sat down next to me. "Okay. I did get you something else, but I'm saving it."

"For what?" I asked. I was worried she was going to say

my birthday, which was four months away. And I didn't feel I should have to wait that long.

"Willy and I want to take you out to dinner and give it to you as a special treat," Grandma said.

This was terrible news. Because I really wanted Willy to just disappear.

"Oh," I said.

Tap. Tap. Tap.

I watched as Grandma tapped on the purple box holding Sylvie's nose hair trimmer.

"What's inside?" Grandma asked.

"Sylvie's birthday present," I said.

"So you want to keep it a mystery until the big reveal," Grandma said.

I nodded.

"Bessica, would you prefer that I not take you to Sylvie's party?" Grandma asked.

She sounded a little bit hurt when she asked me this question. Like maybe I'd be ashamed to have her take me to the party. But that wasn't it. I just didn't know how I felt about Grandma taking me to a party I wasn't invited to.

"You can come," I said.

And I was really surprised to hear myself say this, because it meant that Grandma and I were both going to Sylvie's party even though neither one of us was invited.

"Great!" Grandma said. "You should get moving. We need to leave in an hour."

I looked at my clock. She was right.

"Are you going to dress up?" Grandma asked. "Maybe wear a skirt?"

I shook my head. "No skirt. It's a disco/jungle theme party. I think she's playing a roller-skating game, and I'll need to use my legs and stuff."

"Really?" Grandma asked.

I nodded.

"Well, then I won't wear a skirt either," she said. She winked at me and got up.

"Hey," I said as she was leaving the room. "Willy won't be coming, will he?" I knew my question sounded a little rude, but I didn't like the idea of three uninvited people showing up at Sylvie's birthday party.

"No, Willy went to the auto parts store," Grandma said. "He's fixing a couple of things in the Winnebago."

"Oh," I said. "Cool."

After Grandma left I thought for one second that maybe I should call Sylvie and ask if me and Grandma could come. But then I decided it made a lot more sense just to show up with Grandma and pretend I'd forgotten about all those texts. Or maybe pretend I thought we'd made up. Then the phone rang and I thought maybe Sylvie was calling to invite me at the absolute last minute, so I answered it very quickly.

"This is Bessica," I said.

"This is Alma."

"Oh," I said. I tried not to sound as disappointed as I was.

"Is your grandma or Willy there?"

Grandma didn't have time to have a conversation with Alma. But instead of telling her that, I thought of a better idea. Because I realized that Alma would make a great third wolf! Which was exactly what Willy and Grandma needed so they could break up.

"Willy is at the store, but he'll be back soon. You should come over. He needs help," I said.

"Can't Rhoda help him?" Alma asked.

Rhoda was Grandma's name.

"No," I said. "She's escorting me somewhere." I didn't think I needed to tell Alma all the details of my life.

"I'll see if I can stop by," Alma said.

"Great!"

Then we hung up and I kept getting ready. When I finally came out of my bedroom I was wearing cute jeans, a blue top, and my special sneakers. I'd put in the orange tongues, in honor of Sylvie's jungle theme. Because tigers were orange.

"You look great," Grandma said.

"Yeah," I said.

"Where's your present for Sylvie?" Grandma asked.

It was hidden under my bed. But I didn't tell Grandma that. "Can't your present be from both of us?" I asked.

"Why don't you want to bring your gift?" she asked.

"Um," I said. I worried that if I showed up to the party I wasn't invited to with a lame present for Sylvie, my entire future with Sylvie would be in jeopardy.

"Wait one second," I said as I walked back to my room.

"Don't dawdle," Grandma said. "We don't want to be late."

But I didn't know if that was true.

I walked into my room, but I just couldn't bring myself to get Sylvie's present. I sat on my floor. How had I ended up here? Why did Sylvie have to have such terrible nose hair in the first place? I finally pulled the box out. I couldn't give this to Sylvie. Giving her this gift in front of her friends would be the exact same as complaining to her about her nose hair in front of all her friends. And I would never do that. So I searched my room for something Sylvie would like. But all I found was my own stuff that I wanted to keep forever. So I grabbed a cute tote bag and puffed it up like it had something inside it and figured I'd just lie and say I'd forgotten the present.

I hated lying. But sometimes it made the future feel more hopeful.

Grandma drove Mom's car to the party, and when we got to Sylvie's house there were so many other cars stuffed in the driveway that we had to park along the road.

"Looks like a big party!" Grandma said. "Did you tell Sylvie I'd be home or is she going to be completely surprised to see me?"

I swallowed hard as we walked toward the front door. "She's going to be completely surprised to see you," I said.

Luckily, Sylvie was not standing at the door greeting people as they came in. And the lighting was a little dim. A giant disco ball hung from the ceiling, shooting colors across the walls.

"Mrs. Potaski went all out," Grandma said as we walked in and took off our shoes.

"Yeah," I said. I kept glancing around for people I knew. Uh-oh! I couldn't believe it. Raya Papas was sitting on Sylvie's couch.

"Grandma!" I said. "You'll never guess who's sitting on Sylvie's couch!"

Grandma looked at the couch. "Who is that?"

"It's Raya Papas from my math class. I invited her," I said.

"Sylvie is so sweet to let you invite some of your own friends," Grandma said.

And I didn't exactly know how to explain to Grandma that none of what she'd said was true.

"Bessica!" a voice cheered. "And Rhoda Lefter!"

Nobody called my grandma Rhoda except for a few adults. I glanced around and realized that Mrs. Potaski was the person talking to us.

"I just got back, and I wanted to come and wish Sylvie a very happy birthday," Grandma said.

I watched as Grandma and Mrs. Potaski hugged. I didn't see Sylvie anywhere. Why wasn't she at her own birthday party? And then I saw her. She was sitting next to Raya Papas. How had I missed that? I stopped breathing.

"Do you want to set your tote bag down?" Mrs. Potaski asked.

I nodded.

"Take the present out first," Grandma said, "so we can set it on the gift table."

I took a big breath and held it.

"What's wrong?" Grandma asked.

"I forgot it," I mumbled. Grandma looked very disappointed to learn this.

"No way! Is that Bessica?" a familiar voice called. And it was familiar because it was Sylvie.

I slowly turned and looked at her. And the coolest thing ever happened. She seemed happy. It was amazing. Because I was standing in the middle of her living room as an uninvited party guest and Sylvie was smiling at me. It felt very, very good.

"Hi," I said. "Grandma Lefter came too. But she's not staying for the whole party."

"You're back!" Sylvie yelled as she ran to Grandma and gave her a hug.

Click. Click. Click.

Mrs. Potaski snapped pictures of us looking happy. I hoped all of us stayed looking happy.

After Sylvie finished hugging Grandma, she came over and hugged me. And I was really surprised by what happened next. I heard myself whisper something to Sylvie.

"I'm sorry," I said. "I regret every mean text I sent."

Sylvie stopped hugging me and pulled away from me. She looked me in the eye and smiled. "Yeah," she said. "Me too."

And it felt very good to be forgiven.

"Cool disco ball," I said. "Did it cost a fortune?" I was surprised there wasn't more jungle stuff. No safari hats. No grass skirts. No fake parrots. No monkeys. She didn't even have a single piñata.

Sylvie laughed. "It's a rental. And guess what? In honor of the disco/jungle theme, I invited a special guest."

"Ooh," I said. Because I thought maybe it was a famous disco person.

"A tiger is coming," Sylvie said.

"What?" I said. "That's insane!" Seeing bears behind electric fences seemed reasonable. But bringing a tiger into a house didn't seem smart.

"No. Not a real tiger," Sylvie said. "You know him. He's a mascot."

"No," I said, backing up. *"No."*

"Yes!" Sylvie answered, widening her eyes like a thrilled person. "T.J. the Tiger is coming!"

My world spun faster than the disco ball above me.

"Why?" I asked. "Is he your friend?" Because that seemed evil of her.

"My mom knows his mom, and since my party is a disco/jungle theme it made sense to invite a tiger," Sylvie said. "Plus, he doesn't get invited to many parties. I guess he's not that popular."

"Duh!" I said. "He's the worst." I didn't want to bring up the fact that he wanted to facebomb me, because I didn't even want to say that word. I wondered if he'd try to facebomb me at a party.

"Bessica!" Grandma called. "Did you know that Mrs. Potaski invited a tiger mascot to the party?"

"I just found out," I said.

"He's running a little late," Mrs. Potaski said.

I really hoped the party would get going so we could hurry through it and I could leave without meeting T.J. I wasn't ready to face him. I wasn't even dressed like a bear.

"Maybe you should go talk to Raya. She's nice. And guess what?" Sylvie said. "You forgot to sign her invitation. She didn't even know you were the one who invited her here."

"Oh," I said. I didn't tell Sylvie that I'd done that on purpose.

"Go talk to her," Sylvie said. "Did you know her cousin is an astronaut?"

"No," I said.

I couldn't believe that Sylvie had sat next to Raya Papas for ten minutes and learned the most interesting things ever, and I'd sat next to Raya Papas for weeks and didn't know anything about her except what I could learn from staring at her.

I started to walk toward the couch, but I stopped when Grandma stepped right in front of me.

"I'm headed home. Do you want me to swing back with your present?" she asked.

"No," I said. "Don't do that."

"Okay. I'll pick you up when the party is over. Have a great time. And save me a piece of cake."

"Do you want me to wrap it in napkins?" I asked. Because I'd saved a cupcake for her once like that and it had wrecked the frosting.

"Mrs. Potaski is going to put a piece in some Tupperware for me," Grandma explained.

And as Grandma was leaving, I sort of wished I was leaving too.

"Disco time!" Sylvie yelled. Everybody jumped up and started dancing. The music made the floor throb as the lights spun around the room. *Tiger. Tiger. Tiger.* I couldn't turn my mind off. I was too young to be facebombed at a birthday party.

I decided the best thing to do was to get away from this situation in a hurry. Sylvie and I had made up. I didn't need to stay here and dance. I tripped over somebody's jacket, and the next thing I knew I crashed into the gift table and presents flew everywhere.

"Aah!" I cried. "I'm breaking the presents."

The music stopped, but the disco ball kept spinning. From the floor, I looked up at over a dozen blinking faces.

"Sorry," I said.

"What's wrong?" Sylvie asked.

"I was dancing and I fell," I lied. I didn't want to admit that I was fleeing in fear.

"Why are you dancing on my presents?" Sylvie asked.

"So weird," Raya Papas said.

"No, I was dancing over there and ended up over here," I said. I wanted to convince everybody that I just covered a lot of ground when I danced. "Watch." And I started zooming as wide and far as I could while shaking and shimmying. Admitting that I was afraid of another mascot would make me look lame.

Shimmy. Shimmy. Shake.

Nobody looked amused. They looked freaked out and confused. Then my mind flashed to something Vicki had said. So I unleashed a mojo-building move. "Watch my windmill arms!"

And that was when the worst thing ever happened. That was when Mrs. Potaski entered the room with her triple-layer cream cake and hit my mojo-building windmill arms.

SPLAT!

What a mess. It looked like the cake had exploded. All over Mrs. Potaski. And the carpet. And the gift table. And everybody's shoes.

"My cake!" Sylvie cried.

And when I turned to look at her I saw the most awful thing ever. I saw her sad, sad face bursting into tears. And I saw Malory Mahoney the Big Plastic Phony putting her arm around her. And I wished that I could have been the one to be putting my arm around Sylvie. But I wasn't because I had just windmill-armed her mom and her birthday cake.

Knock. Knock. Knock.

The person at the door didn't wait for anybody to

answer it. It swung open and there stood Grandma. She looked very shocked when she saw the exploded cake. I rushed toward her and put my hands out in a begging way. I think I wanted forgiveness.

"I decided to bring Sylvie's present for you after all," Grandma asked. "This party looks out of control."

"Oh, Grandma," I said. "I unleashed a mojo-building countermove and it damaged the cake. And now I need to leave before I get facebombed by a tiger."

"Bessica Lefter ruined the disco/jungle party," Raya Papas said.

"Oh my," Grandma said.

I covered my eyes with my hands, but it didn't really improve the situation. Why had I invited one of the meanest people I knew to this party?

Grandma was still holding Sylvie's present, so she walked it over to the gifts scattered on the floor and set the purple box down next to a cute pink one.

"Thanks," I said. But really, I couldn't believe that Grandma had returned to the birthday party and brought Sylvie the battery-operated nose hair trimmer. First, Grandma didn't belong at a tween disco/jungle party. Second, Sylvie was going to open her gift and hate me forever now.

"I want to leave," I said. "And never come back. And possibly change my name and move."

"Everything is going to be okay," Grandma said.

"This party is weird," a girl said.

"Was all that supposed to happen?" another girl asked. "Was it part of the entertainment?"

"Can we leave?" I asked Grandma.

"Whose grandma keeps coming to the party?" a girl asked.

Grandma sort of looked like she didn't know what to do. "Do you want to stay and sort this out?"

Mrs. Potaski was lifting big chunks of cake up off the floor and setting them on paper plates. Did she really think people were going to eat that? Because I sure wasn't.

"Not really," I said.

"Don't you think you should say goodbye to Sylvie?" Grandma asked.

I turned to look at Sylvie, but Malory was still hugging her and whispering really nice things in her ear. I glanced at Raya Papas. This wasn't how I wanted things to go at all.

"I am so sorry," I said. "I am the sorriest sorry person you've ever met." And then I rushed past Grandma and grabbed my tote bag and ran out the door and raced to the car and got inside and slammed the door and closed my eyes as tight as I could.

It didn't take long for Grandma to climb in beside me. "I know things feel horrible, but this is just a low point. Things will start improving very soon."

I flipped around to face Grandma. "Sylvie has ridiculously hairy nostrils and so I bought her a battery-operated nose hair trimmer and that's what was inside the box you brought."

Grandma looked stunned. "Why would you give Sylvie that?"

"I thought I was doing her a favor," I offered.

"Bessica, Bessica, Bessica," Grandma said.

"Is my low point going to get lower?" I asked.

"Probably," she said. "It's always a bad idea to buy people grooming devices."

"Yeah," I said.

"But you're a good egg. This should sort itself out." Grandma didn't sound totally convinced.

"Do you think Sylvie will forgive me?" I asked.

There was a little bit of a pause.

"You two have a lot of history," Grandma said.

"That's true," I said. "But some of it's bad."

Grandma pulled the car into our driveway and slid the gearshift into park.

"Bessica," Grandma said, sounding very serious. "I promise you that while this may feel like the worst problem you'll ever face in your life, it isn't."

It was almost as if Grandma knew that T.J. planned to facebomb me at the game.

"I thought being a mascot would make my life easier," I said.

"What does being a mascot have to do with the cake debacle?" Grandma asked as she turned off the ignition.

"Everything," I said. I climbed out of the car and dragged myself into my house and down the hallway to my room.

"You're back already?" my mom called from the kitchen.

But I didn't answer. I climbed into bed in my cricket-ridden room and stared at Bianca and tried to keep my mind from replaying the terrible events of the day. But my mind wouldn't stop. I closed my eyes and saw my windmill arms meeting Sylvie's cake. *Whirl. Whirl. Whirl. Splat. Splat. Splat.* What a gigantic disaster.

THINGS THAT WILL DESTROY ALL HAPPINESS IN MIDDLE SCHOOL

1. Orange food
2. Triangle crushes
3. Bucking cows
4. Impulsive biting
5. Jury of your peers

CHAPTER

I got up and had breakfast with Mom, Grandma, and Willy, and we didn't talk about the disco/jungle party fiasco at all. Partly, I think this was because my mom didn't know about it yet. I really appreciated Grandma's not bringing it up.

"Your food collage is due today, right?" my mom asked.

"Yeah," I said.

"Can I see it?" my mom asked.

I wasn't sure I wanted to show my mom my food collage, because it had a few candy bar pictures on it and a mountainous amount of cheese puffs. Did I want her to find out that one-third of my food collage was junk food?

"I've already rolled it up with a rubber band," I said. "Can I show it to you after I get a grade?"

My mom frowned. "Are you hiding something?"

Then Grandma spoke and rescued me. "These eggs are so delicious they almost stop my heart."

"Mmm," I added.

"Very good indeed," Willy said.

I glanced at Willy. I could not believe he was sitting at our table eating eggs with us. Didn't he miss New Mexico? Didn't his friends and family who lived in New Mexico want him to go back there? I sure did.

"Bessica," my mom said in a chirpy voice. "Before I forget, I bought you a pair of wicking socks."

I just stared at her and continued to eat my eggs.

"They pull moisture away from your feet and prevent blisters," she explained. "I bought them for game day."

Game day. I had very mixed feelings about that day.

"Thank you," I said. Then I stood up very quickly so I could gather my things and catch the bus.

"Willy and I wear wicking socks when we go caving," Grandma said. "In addition to preventing blisters, they also reduce chafing and fungus."

"Gross," I said. "I don't have those problems." It was hard to hear the word *fungus* and not think of Sylvie. And it was hard to think of Sylvie and not remember ruining her birthday.

"Here they are," my mom said, lifting up a pair of gray socks.

"Okay," I said. "I don't need them now. I need to go to school."

"You're cranky," my mom said.

"Let her be," Grandma said.

I sure hoped Willy didn't say anything, because I was getting madder and madder that he was even in our kitchen.

"I'm going to be late!" I huffed. I grabbed my things and hurried out the door.

Once I got to school, things got a little bit worse. Because word had gotten out about T.J.'s desire to face-bomb me, and everybody was talking about it. Annabelle raced up to me right away. "Is it true that you're going to get attacked by the other school's mascot?"

That was a very unpleasant thing to hear. "I hope not," I said, unloading my backpack.

"I can't believe T.J. thinks he can get away with this!" Annabelle said. "I'm going to tell everybody in social sciences."

"Wait, wait," I said. But Annabelle was already gone. I wasn't sure I wanted her to tell people about this in social sciences.

After I got to nutrition, I sat and waited anxiously for Mrs. Mounds to show up. I felt a little self-conscious showing everybody what I'd been eating. I mean, how many cheese puffs had they eaten in the last two weeks? I had a feeling some people might not have been completely honest. When psycho-bully Redge arrived, he clomped into the classroom with his collage and sat down behind me and demanded his daily pen. But I put my head down and didn't respond.

"I am waiting for my pen," he said in a calm voice.

"Yeah," I said. "Wait longer."

Then he poked me. I didn't know what was wrong with him. Didn't he have any manners? I flipped around to snap at him, but when I did I saw him and his snotty face and it intimidated me and so I gave him his pen.

"Thanks," he said.

I looked at my collage. All the food I'd eaten for two weeks swam around on the page. In an effort to add more orange to my collage I'd added too much. I wasn't embarrassed by my cheese puffs, or macaroni and cheese, or carrots, or squash, or sweet potatoes, or mango smoothie, but I was suddenly surprised by the lack of green food. Especially when I saw other people's collages. Wow. Were the people in my class really eating that much salad?

I studied mine again. I'd drawn a picture of myself in the center, but I wasn't very good at drawing and the picture didn't really look like me. It looked like a generic person with short hair. I wondered how many art classes

I would have to take before I became good at drawing. I stared some more at my collage and my generic hair. In the coming days I was going to have to make a decision about my pixie cut. Trim it? Or let it grow? Hmm. But I didn't have much time to think about this because I felt another poke. I turned around.

"Do you want to see my collage?" psycho-bully Redge asked me.

"Not really," I said. Then I started to flip back around.

"I think you'll find it interesting," he added.

So I turned back around. And he pointed to a picture of Two-Taste Teton donuts.

"Were those the donuts Cola swiped from me?" I asked.

"Yep," Redge said. "They were delicious."

And I didn't understand why Redge wanted to make me feel bad. That was the thing I didn't understand about bullies. They got joy out of hurting other people's feelings. Jerks.

"I've heard the rumor," Redge said.

"Yeah," I said. But I didn't turn back around.

"You're in trouble. T.J. the Tiger is a psycho mascot," he said.

I didn't say anything.

"Psycho. Psycho. Psycho," he said.

The way he said that made me feel very frightened. I didn't even want to stay at school and hand in my food collage anymore. But I did. I sat through nutrition. And English. And math. And I'd really hoped that Raya Papas would talk to me and maybe make me feel better about what had happened at the birthday party, but she didn't. At least, not until the end of class, when she said, "Giving your friend a nose hair trimmer is crazy." And I wanted to justify why I'd done that. But I didn't. Because Grandma had pretty much nailed it when she told me that giving people grooming devices is always a bad idea.

"Who are you eating lunch with?" I asked.

"My friends," Raya Papas said. "And none of them would give me a nose hair trimmer. Because *they* are all normal."

Then Raya walked away and I went to my locker and dumped off my stuff and headed to meet up with Annabelle, Lola, Dee, and Macy.

"Let's consider the big picture," Lola said as we sat down to eat. "If you do get facebombed, you're going to be the most famous mascot our school has ever seen."

"It's not worth it," Macy said.

Dee nodded.

"What if it hurts?" I asked.

"Of course it will hurt!" Annabelle said.

"Maybe he's joking," I said.

I wished I believed that.

"Mascots always tease that they're going to fight the

other mascot. But they never do. They're all talk," Macy said.

Then Jasper walked up to our table and Annabelle quit breathing.

"Are you talking about T.J.?" Jasper asked.

Nobody said anything. We all just stared at Jasper. Hard.

"I'm here to give you the inside scoop," he said. Then Jasper guzzled the rest of his milk, set the empty carton on our table, and squashed the container with his hand. "That kid is all business."

Annabelle covered her mouth like she was shocked to learn this. Also I think she was trying to flirt with Jasper.

"Doesn't anybody remember Track and Field Days last year and what he did to Robin Lord?" Jasper said.

I gasped. "What did he do to Robin Lord?" She was so nice. One of the nicest people I'd ever met. It was like a marshmallow met a puppy and became a person.

"Track and Field Day last year. Robin Lord was getting ready for the relay race and he taped a sign to her back that said TEAM POOPER."

"That's terrible," I said.

"It gets worse. Everybody was laughing at Robin when she ran and she didn't know why, and it was so distracting that when she passed the baton she dropped it and tripped. The team lost and she landed on her face."

"That's why her eye twitches," Macy said.

"No!" I'd noticed that Robin Lord's eye twitched, but I had no idea it was because she'd been ambushed with a TEAM POOPER sign.

"You need to take him down," Annabelle said. "And the whole school will worship you."

"That's a great idea," Lola said. "You should facebomb T.J."

"Do it!" Jasper said.

But I didn't even know how to do that. "I can't even think about that right now. I just want to finish my lunch," I said.

"Think it over," Jasper said. "And let me know if I can help."

"Thanks for stopping by," I said.

"Yeah," Annabelle said.

Jasper smiled at Annabelle. And he smiled at me. Then he left.

"Have you two made up?" I asked.

"Mostly," Annabelle said. "But things still feel weird."

"Duh," Macy said. "He's a guy."

It was always a little surprising how accurate Macy's observations were.

By the time I got to geography, the new rumor was that I was going to facebomb T.J. And by the time I got to PE, people were in such a frenzy that three girls came up to me and said that they wanted to help me clobber T.J. at the game. They said they knew jujitsu.

I didn't know what to say. So I told them what I knew about the football field policy. "Spectators aren't allowed on the turf."

I figured they were just venting.

But when I got to my locker and opened it and a flood of notes came tumbling out, all telling me that it was my job to punish T.J., I began to realize that if I could stand up to T.J. and also avoid getting facebombed, I would become super-famous at my school. And wasn't that really why I'd tried out for mascot anyway? Honestly, wasn't that the entire point of middle school?

CHAPTER

Worrying about getting facebombed zapped all my energy. My mind felt so fuzzy as I rode the bus home that I couldn't daydream about good stuff, such as cheering like a champion at Friday's game, or my reunion with gorgeous Noll Beck when I gave him back his lizard. My mind was stuck on T.J. *Jerk. Jerk. Jerk.* Tragically, as I stepped off the bus, the first person I saw was Willy. He and Grandma were sitting outside in the driveway on lawn chairs.

"How was your day?" Grandma asked.

But I didn't want to talk about my day.

"Why are you sitting out here?" I asked.

"We just washed the chairs and were getting ready to

store them again and decided to take a load off," Grandma said.

I couldn't help noticing that there were two lawn chairs and two of them and no place for me to sit.

"Do you want to sit on my lap?" Grandma asked.

I looked at her lap. Had she forgotten that I was turning twelve in four months?

"I need to drain the refrigerator," Willy said. "Why don't you take my seat?"

So Willy got up and I took his seat.

"Did you turn in your nutrition collage?" Grandma asked.

"I did," I said. "And I was called on to present it too."

"Did you stand up in front of the whole class?"

"Yeah," I said. "Other than my love of cheese puffs and orange food, I was one of the more normal eaters in there. Also, I should eat more salad."

"As should we all," Grandma said. "Did anybody have something exotic in their collage? Like octopus or cactus?"

I made a gagging sound so Grandma would understand that I never wanted to eat octopus or cactus. "Some kids eat a lot of canned foods. And a few people's families catch fish in reservoirs that might be polluted."

"Sounds like an informative assignment," Grandma said.

"I guess," I said. "Only I didn't want to learn that

people in my class ate polluted fish. Their collages made me sad."

"You're very sensitive," Grandma said.

And I turned and looked at her when she said this. "I really am," I replied. Then I saw something weird in the grass. "What's that weird thing?" I pointed to what looked like a jumbo washcloth attached to a stick.

"That's Alma's," Grandma said. "It's a cleaning system she brought over for Willy to borrow to wash the Winnebago."

I nodded. I was happy to hear that the potential third wolf was stopping by and leaving stuff for Willy. I glanced at the motor home. "That thing is filthy."

"We've been driving across the country. It's supposed to get dirty."

When Grandma said the words *driving across the country,* it made me remember how much I had missed her when she was gone. "I hope you don't ever leave again."

"Is something weighing on you?" Grandma asked. "Did something happen at school?"

And I felt like telling Grandma every single thing in the world that was weighing on me. But I didn't want to bum her out. So I only told her a couple of things.

"Raya Papas told me that Sylvie opened her nose hair trimmer."

"How did that gift strike her?" Grandma asked.

I shrugged.

"When do you think you'll reach out to her?" Grandma asked.

But the thought of calling or texting Sylvie made my insides quiver in real pain. Because I felt horrible about what had happened. And I didn't know whether I would forgive me if I were Sylvie. And if I couldn't imagine forgiving me, how could I expect Sylvie to?

While I was thinking, I felt something tickle my leg. It was an ant. I slapped it with my hand and squished it.

"Bessica," Grandma said. "You didn't have to kill it."

"Sure I did," I said. "It was crawling on me."

"Bessica, Bessica, Bessica," Grandma said. "You're so impulsive." And then she didn't say anything.

We sat and listened to the wind start to blow. Banging sounds came out of the motor home as Willy drained the refrigerator. I knew I should practice being a bear. But I was just too tired.

"I better get in there and help him," Grandma said.

I wasn't ready for her to leave.

"I'm nervous about Friday's game," I said.

"It's normal to be nervous. But I'm sure you'll do an excellent job," Grandma said.

"Yeah," I mumbled.

"Willy and I will both be there," she said. "And so will your parents and so will Alma."

I was actually happy to hear that Alma would be there. Because the more time the third wolf spent with the wolf couple, the easier it was going to be to make Willy fall in love with the third wolf and leave Grandma alone. But I didn't necessarily want all these people to watch me get facebombed. Or, in the best-case scenario, I didn't want all these people to watch me facebomb T.J. Because I would probably do it all wrong.

Just then, Alma drove by and she honked at Grandma and Grandma waved back like she was thrilled.

"Do you like Alma?" I asked. Because I didn't want Grandma to lose a friend when Willy and Alma ran off together.

"She's building a new life. She needs friends," Grandma said. "She's growing her circle."

"But if you just met her on the street you probably wouldn't like her. Right?" I asked.

"I wouldn't say that," she said.

"Ouch!" Willy called from the motor home. "I can't get this blasted tubing to come apart."

I looked at Grandma. I didn't want her to leave me. Couldn't Willy handle the tubing by himself? Couldn't he do anything without Grandma? She pushed off her chair and stood up.

"Grandma?" I asked. "What if when I'm cheering at the game I'm terrible? I mean, not a little terrible. But totally truly very terrible? Or what if something terrible happens?"

"There's no way you will be terrible. And nothing terrible is going to happen," she said. "It's a game. People go for the fun of it."

"What if I let people down?" I asked.

"Who could you possibly be letting down?"

I looked at the clouds inching across the sky. I didn't want to tell Grandma about all the facebombing that might take place. But it was sort of like she could read my mind.

"Do you want to know one of the key things to living a happy life?" Grandma asked me.

"Of course," I said.

"Do what makes you happy in a manner that doesn't hurt anyone else," she said.

"Okay," I said. I felt myself holding back tears. "Thanks for sharing that with me."

"Happiness isn't something you chase, Bessica," Grandma said. "It's just the way you feel."

I'd never thought about the fact that I was chasing happiness.

"I still haven't finished my Arctic collage," I said.

"Why not?" Grandma asked.

I shrugged. "I already did a collage. For nutrition."

"Collage fatigue?" Grandma said, laughing a little.

I nodded. Then I felt my phone buzz and I looked at it. Ooh. "I have to take this. It's Annabelle. I give her great advice."

Annabelle: Jasper is driving me nuts!
Me: I can't really talk. I have to make a stupid collage.
Annabelle: I thought you finished your collage and it turned out *super*-orange.
Me: (Sigh) Different collage.

I felt Grandma touch my arm. "Invite your friend over to help you."

I shook my head. I didn't think Annabelle would be much help. If she came over, all she'd do was talk about Jasper and distract me.

Annabelle: Is that your mom? Did she just invite me over?
Me: No.

Then Grandma touched my arm again. "Willy and I can pick her up. Or drop her off if that's a problem."

I shook my head again. Didn't Grandma know what it meant when I shook my head? I covered my phone with my hand and whispered, "Bad idea. We'll need to ask Mom first."

"Your mom and dad aren't here," Grandma said. "They went on a drive to Jackson Hole. They've having a date night."

I kept my phone covered. "But they don't have those."

Annabelle: Is that your grandma? I'd love to meet her.

Then Grandma did something crazy. She leaned into my phone and said, "I'd love to meet you too, Annabelle."

Annabelle: I'm on my way!

Annabelle hung up and I hung up and then I stared at Grandma. "I might never finish my collage now."

"Sure you will," Grandma said. "You'll be inspired by the company of your friend."

Sometimes it was like Grandma and I didn't even live on the same planet. "I don't think that's true. Annabelle isn't even taking geography. And for my assignment I'm supposed to answer the question 'What would you see if you went to the Arctic?' But when I try to imagine what I'd see, all I picture is snow, and my blank piece of poster board works for that."

"Sounds like you've got an interesting project on your hands," Grandma said.

"That's a lie." I leaned back in my chair and stared at the awful Winnebago. "One collage a year is plenty." I closed my eyes. Mr. Hoser and Mrs. Mounds shouldn't both have been allowed to assign such terrible identical homework. I felt tortured. I turned and looked at Grandma. "There should be a rule against terrible identical homework. Teachers should be required to be more imaginative."

"Don't bash teachers. They've got tough jobs," Grandma said. "Let me get Willy. We'll cook a motivating meal for you and your friend."

Motivating or not, I did not want to eat Willy's cooking.

And I did not want Annabelle to come to my house and obsess about Jasper.

And I did not want to make a second collage.

And I did not want to get facebombed.

"Does Willy know how to make pizza?" I asked.

Grandma's hearing was as sensitive as a bat's. She called to me from the Winnebago, "Willy makes fantastic pizza!"

"I actually make far better calzones!" Willy added.

I didn't say anything back. I wasn't sure a calzone would improve anything for anyone. Especially me.

CHAPTER

Annabelle arrived excited and ready to chat. Also, she was wearing clothes that looked like pajamas.

"Are you spending the night?" I asked as I led her to my room. Because it was a school night and I didn't think that was wise or allowed.

"I like wearing comfy clothes," Annabelle said. Then she didn't comment on my green lizard or offer to help me with my collage at all or bring up the fact that I should be practicing my cheers. She launched into Jasper chat. "He texted me earlier today and asked if he could visit us at lunch tomorrow. Isn't that weird? What do you think it means?"

I spritzed Bianca with some water and then sat down and stared at my poster board. "I don't think it's weird. He likes talking to you."

"Right," Annabelle said, plopping down next to me. "But he's never texted and asked for permission before. I think his feelings for me are deepening. What do you think?"

I didn't tell Annabelle what I thought. Because I thought she was acting like a crazy person. "Maybe we should help my grandma and Willy make calzones."

I didn't want to help them, but talking to Annabelle was driving me nuts. When we got to the kitchen Willy and Grandma were listening to terrible country music about people getting divorces and horses running wild and cowboys missing other cowboys who were either dead or in prison.

"This music is depressing," I said.

"Really?" Willy asked, turning the station. "It lifts me up."

"I like it too," Grandma said. "Shows human perseverance."

Willy found a station playing popular music with lots of drums that normal people listened to and I felt much better.

"Do you girls like pepperoni?" Willy asked as he tossed a slab of dough in the air and twirled it.

"I do!" Annabelle said.

Annabelle and I sat at the breakfast bar while Grandma and Willy whipped up dinner.

"Do you want tomatoes in your salad?" Grandma asked us as she chopped the life out of a head of lettuce.

"I want information about the Arctic. So I can properly locate pictures and glue them to my poster board," I said.

"What's the theme again?" Grandma asked.

I couldn't believe Grandma had forgotten my theme already.

"I have to make a collage that answers the following question: 'If I went to the Arctic, what would I see?'"

"Willy has been to Barrow, Alaska," Grandma said. "It's the northernmost city in the United States."

"That's amazing!" Annabelle said.

"That's cool," I said. But I didn't really care.

"I've got some good travel books about the Arctic," Willy said.

"You'd lend Bessica your books?" Grandma asked.

"I'd love to!" Willy said.

"Your Arctic books are currently inside your Winnebago?" I asked. Because it felt like Willy should have told me this as soon as he'd heard about my collage.

"You can't cut them up," Willy said. "But you can use them for information."

"What a huge coincidence, Bessica!" Annabelle gushed. "You are so lucky Willy is here."

I could not believe Annabelle had said that. My ears rang in horror.

"I should not be making calzones or an Arctic collage. I should be practicing my bear cheers," I said under my breath. But then there wasn't time to do either of those things, because we needed to hang out with Willy and Grandma until dinner was ready.

After we ate our calzones and salad, Willy gave me his books and Annabelle and I went to my bedroom.

"Hit me with an arrow!" Annabelle said.

"What?" I asked. I unrolled my poster board and put shoes on the corners to keep it from curling up.

"It's a saying related to Cupid. God of love. Son of Venus," Annabelle said. "Jasper texted me again. He wants to bring dessert for me tomorrow. A special cookie."

I looked at her but didn't say anything.

"He's basically asking me to be his girlfriend," Annabelle said. "Isn't he?"

I didn't agree or disagree. "You should call and ask Lola about that." Lola liked to analyze boy stuff more than I did. And I needed to finish my collage so I could practice my cheers a little.

I stared at my books. "If I went to the Arctic all I would see was snow. Doesn't Mr. Hoser know that already?"

Knock. Knock. Knock.

"How are things going in there?" Grandma asked.

"Fantastic!" Annabelle said.

"Awful," I said.

"Aren't Willy's books helping?" Grandma asked.

Willy had given me two terrible books. *Silent Snow,* which was very big and talked about how all the world's pollutants had traveled to the Arctic and turned it and every single polar bear toxic. And *The Complete Idiot's Guide to the Arctic and Antarctic,* which I didn't really want to open because I found the title a little insulting.

"I'm just going to Google the Arctic and print out some pictures," I said. "Research is hard."

Annabelle didn't say anything because she was busy texting Lola.

Grandma frowned at me. "This sounds like a delightful assignment. You get to read about polar bears and ice floes and ringed seals."

"Yeah, yeah, yeah," I said.

"Do you think it would help to watch a movie?" Grandma asked.

I sat up straight. "Probably." I liked watching movies with Grandma.

"Movies are the best," Annabelle said as she furiously punched buttons on her phone.

"Willy, bless his heart, went to pick up a movie about polar bears," Grandma said. "I think he's hoping that you two might bond over the Arctic."

"Wow," I said. "That's weird." Because I could imagine Willy bonding over the Arctic with Mr. Hoser, but I couldn't imagine Willy bonding over the Arctic with me. Ever.

"Willy is the best," Annabelle said.

I really regretted that Annabelle was in my bedroom right now.

"Would you do me a favor?" Grandma asked.

"Yes," I said.

"Would you give Willy a chance?" she asked. "I love Willy. I want you two to get along."

I couldn't believe Grandma loved Willy. She was going to be devastated when he ran off with Alma.

"I *am* giving him a chance," I said.

Then I heard the front door slam.

"I got the Arctic DVD!" Willy yelled.

So Grandma and me and Annabelle and Willy gathered in the living room and popped in the DVD.

Tap. Tap. Tap.

"What's that sound?" Grandma asked.

"Annabelle texting," I said.

"I just need to ask Dee one more question," Annabelle said.

"I thought you were texting Lola," I said.

"She got a thumb cramp," Annabelle said.

I looked at Grandma and rolled my eyes.

"Let's put our electronics away and concentrate on the film," Grandma said.

Tap. Tap. Tap.

Annabelle looked devastated.

"I'm trying to figure out whether or not I have a boyfriend," Annabelle said.

I rolled my eyes big-time at that.

"Seems like the sort of thing best figured out face to face," Grandma said. Then she cranked up the volume.

The film started off showing icebergs and polar bears, and then a narrator came on and informed us that in one hundred years the Arctic would be totally melted.

"This is bumming me out," I said.

"My grandma thinks the world will end in less than twenty-five years," Annabelle said.

"Let's just watch the movie," Grandma said. "National Geographic made it. That means it's high quality."

"Look. There's a lot of things to put on your poster," Willy said.

And Willy was right. Because after a couple of minutes the screen was flooded with stuff. "Ooh," I said. "The Arctic has birds? I didn't know that." I kept watching. "And seals! And polar bears. And walruses. And biologists on snowmobiles with fur hats and dogs."

"Those look like Labrador retrievers," Grandma said.

"Cool," I said. "I can find them on the Internet."

"Should you be taking notes?" Grandma asked me.

I tapped my head. "No. I'm great at storing information."

Willy chuckled at this. And it didn't really bother me. Because I was grateful that he'd found such a cool DVD for us to watch.

Buzz. Buzz. Buzz.

We all looked at Annabelle.

"Sorry," she said.

I watched her catch a quick glance of her screen. "It's a text from Jasper!" she whispered.

I started watching the movie again. The camera was underwater, showing everything that lived below the ice. "What's that thing?" I yelled. I saw the weirdest animal ever. It looked like a seal with a huge spike on its head.

"It's a narwhal," Grandma said. "Hasn't your teacher mentioned them?"

"No," I said. "He has not." Which was a big surprise to me, because they were the freakiest animals I'd ever seen, and if Mr. Hoser had mentioned them, I bet the entire class would have become much more interested in the Arctic.

"I thought I saw a narwhal once," Willy said. "But it was a beluga whale."

It would have been a much better story if Willy had actually seen a narwhal. "Too bad," I said, and I kept watching the DVD.

"Only the male has the tusk," Willy said. "It's a tooth."

"Ouch," I said. Because the narrator said the tusk could grow to be nine feet long.

"When I get home I'm going to text Jasper about this," Annabelle said. Then, using her phone, she took a picture of me. "I'm sending that to Lola. Your hair looks so cute right now."

But I worried that Annabelle was overtexting. Jasper. Lola. Everybody.

"Look at the seals," Grandma said.

"I've seen hundreds in real life," Willy said.

I was surprised to hear this. "I thought you were a welder," I said. I didn't know why he'd see that many seals and a beluga whale. Did he weld aquariums?

"Before my wife passed we were quite the globe-trotters," Willy said.

I glanced at Grandma. I wondered if it hurt her feelings that Willy was talking about his wife.

"Here's some more narwhals," Annabelle said.

I listened closely to the DVD narrator. "'Narwhals' chief predators are killer whales.'" Then a picture of a killer whale eating something bloody flashed across the screen.

"No! Not the narwhal!" I said. I had not been expecting to see blood in the Arctic. Then the documentary showed killer whales chasing what appeared to be more narwhals.

"Those guys are goners," Annabelle said.

"Actually, because they don't have dorsal fins, they can swim right under the surface of the ice," Willy said. "Killer whales have huge dorsal fins and can't do that. So the narwhals might have a shot. *If* they can make it back to the ice."

"Go narwhals! Go narwhals!" I said.

"Don't forget to breathe," Grandma said.

"I'm breathing," I said.

"Oh! Oh! They made it," Annabelle said. "I'm going to text Jasper and tell him."

And none of us objected to this. Because stopping Annabelle from texting Jasper took way too much energy.

Watching the narwhals almost get eaten made me think a lot about T.J. Because he was like a killer whale. Out for blood. And I needed to outsmart him. Or else I'd get slaughtered.

"It's over," Grandma said, pushing a button and returning us to the main menu. "Do you want to watch the bonus footage?"

"My mom just texted me that she's parked out front," Annabelle said.

Honk. Honk. Honk.

"That's her," Annabelle said, leaping up off the couch and grabbing her coat. "Thanks for everything!"

I walked to the door and gave Annabelle a hug. "Good

luck with your collage," she said. "And that crazy lizard. This was so much fun!"

But Annabelle only hugged me with one arm because she was texting somebody with her other hand.

"That girl sure likes that Jasper," Willy said.

But I didn't want Willy to judge my friends.

"I should probably get started on my collage," I said.

"Where will you get the pictures?" Grandma asked. "You can't cut up Willy's books."

"I have some magazines," I said. "I won't cut up Willy's books." Even though I'd already seen some excellent pictures of polar bears in his copy of *Silent Snow*.

Once I focused, it only took me an hour to cut out my pictures. I also went online and found some, which was allowed, as long as we had some other sources. I used Willy's books to help me make more of a story out of my collage. For instance, since polar bears eat and drink lots of pollutants, they've become some of the most toxic creatures on the planet. To reflect this, I had them dripping black and purple toxic droplets onto the snow. And when I attached my pictures of the killer whales, I added blood around their mouths. And when I added a narwhal, I placed a thought bubble next to it that said I have decades' worth of chemicals trapped in my blubber. Because just like the polar bears, narwhals are toxic too. I worried a little bit that my collage was looking a little depressing. Especially when I wrote next to a group of walruses, *Don't eat me. I am contaminated.* It was a bummer that the Arctic was in such bad shape.

Knock. Knock. Knock.

"Status check," Grandma said.

"It's done," I said.

Grandma stared at it and blinked. "Wow. That looks pretty grim. Why are your polar bears sweating? Is that meant to suggest global warming?"

I shook my head. "They're so toxic they're dripping chemicals," I explained.

Then Willy poked his head in the door. "Can I see it?"

I lifted it above my head.

"You really nailed the direness of the situation," Willy said.

I smiled. "Do you think I'll get an A?"

"That all depends on how Mr. Hoser feels about direness," Grandma said.

I released a huge yawn.

"I'd give you an A," Willy said.

I smiled at Willy. Then I yawned again.

"You better rest up. Tomorrow is the big game!" Grandma said. "Do you wear a special outfit to school to show team spirit?"

I shook my head. "Just jeans and a cute top." Then I

stretched. "I wish I could wear my bear paws. Do you think the school would let me?"

"You don't want to walk around in your bear paws all day," Grandma said.

But I sort of did.

"Brush your teeth and get ready for bed," Grandma said. "And try not to think about the toxic Arctic."

"I won't," I said. But that wasn't true. Because after I'd assembled my collage I'd grown very worried about all the animals storing chemicals in their blubber. Were they ever going to be okay? How do you get pollution out of a seal or a narwhal once they have it inside them? What about the baby polar bears?

I brushed my teeth. And swished some fluoride. Then I changed into my pajamas and crawled into bed.

I hoped Mom and Dad were having a fun date night. I hoped Annabelle had stopped texting Jasper. And I hoped Noll Beck hadn't gotten injured on his horse trip. I really wanted to text him. Maybe tomorrow. I flicked off Bianca's light.

"Oh, gorgeous Noll Beck," I whispered. "I want you to come back the same way you left. In one gorgeous piece." Then I felt something on me and almost screamed because I thought it was a cricket. But it wasn't. I sighed. "I hope when Noll gets back I'm still in one piece too."

CHAPTER

I felt like I was going to puke. The game was tonight and my entire life was on the line. Literally. That morning, I got up and rushed to the computer. I needed to find out what it meant to be facebombed. I couldn't believe that I hadn't looked it up yet. I guessed that was what happened when you had multiple assigned collages. You did your homework online, but you forgot you could solve your problems that way too.

"What are you doing, Bessica?" my dad asked.

I turned off the computer before I had a chance to find out what *facebomb* meant. I was supposed to ask for permission before I went online.

"Nothing," I said. "How was Jackson Hole?"

"Your mom and I had a pretty wonderful time. We should do that more often," he said.

But I didn't know if I agreed with that.

My dad stood in the den area in his bathrobe looking tired and awful. I was glad I didn't look that way in the morning or everybody at school would laugh at me.

"Are you checking your email?" he asked.

I shook my head. "I check that at school. I was doing research before the big game."

My dad smiled, yawned, and scratched his neck.

"I'm going to Flip-cam the whole thing! I can't wait to see you in action. *Grrr.*" He lifted his hands up and curved his fingers to make paws. I hoped he didn't do that in front of people from my school.

Once I was all dressed and ready and was sitting at the table eating, I was overcome by feelings of fear, dread, and freaked-outness.

"Why isn't Grandma eating with us?" I asked.

My mom and dad looked at each other.

"Aren't you happy I'm here?" my dad asked. Because it was unusual that he got up this early to eat with us.

"Grandma likes Willy more than she likes me," I said. And I didn't even know I felt that way until I heard myself say it.

"They were up late and they're sleeping in. Love isn't

a contest," my mom said. "One person can love a lot of people."

"Maybe. But you can't eat breakfast with one person while you're living in a Winnebago with another person and sleeping late," I explained. "You've got to choose who you love more."

"You're thinking about it all wrong," my mother said.

"No I'm not," I replied.

Getting my things and catching the bus didn't make me feel any better. Because I had to walk past the Winnebago. And instead of banging on the side of it and telling Grandma and Willy that they'd hurt my feelings by missing my game-day pancake breakfast, I sneaked past it as quietly as I could.

All day long I walked through the hallways so anxious that I felt like I was buzzing. It seemed like everybody I passed wanted me to take T.J. down.

"Kick him in the butt!"

"Smack him hard!"

"Say rude things about his mother!"

I couldn't walk down the hallway without people offering me advice. It was sort of confusing, because I knew it was wrong to want to humiliate and/or injure the opposing team's mascot. But it was also very tempting.

Walk. Walk. Walk.

I pulled my rolled-up poster board out of my locker and

flicked the rubber band back. It made a ferocious snapping sound.

"Ooh!" somebody behind me said. "You should torment T.J. by snapping him with rubber bands."

But I just blinked at this suggestion, because our costumes had too much fur for that to work.

As soon as I entered geography, it was clear to me that I might not have completed my collage correctly. Because everybody else had pictures that made the Arctic look like a very frozen and lovely place. None of their polar bears or killer whales looked toxic at all. They looked healthy and ready to attack people and seals and each other. I sat at my desk and tried to hold my poster board edges flat. But they kept curling up.

"What happened to your collage?" Robin Lord asked me.

"Nothing," I said. When I looked at her I saw her eye twitch, and it made my stomach flip.

"But it looks like everything is dying," Robin said.

I stared at my collage. Then I looked at Robin. "The Arctic got polluted. And now those pollutants are stuck inside most of the animals' blubber."

"That's awful," Robin said. "Is that why your polar bears are sweating black spots?"

I nodded. "They measure the level of pollutants inside of polar bears by extracting nonessential teeth and running tests on them."

"That's triple awful," Robin said. "Hey. What's that?"

Her eye twitched so much that I couldn't look at her while I talked. "It's a narwhal."

"And did the toxic Arctic make it grow a mutant horn?"

"No. All male narwhals grow those. It's a tooth in their bottom jaw." I was going to explain more, but I didn't. Because a tall adult shadow fell across my collage. It was Mr. Hoser.

"Wow," Mr. Hoser said. Then he took his index finger and pointed at my distraught walruses. "They look terrible."

"Yes," I said. "They are very, very toxic. I read all about it in *Silent Snow*."

Mr. Hoser's eyes got big. "You read *Silent Snow* for this assignment?"

"Yes," I said. Which wasn't the total truth. But it was part of the truth. Because I'd read part of the book. And that seemed acceptable.

I watched Mr. Hoser trace his finger along my ice floes. "It's so strange," he said. Then he moved his finger to my narwhals. "And so sad."

"Yeah," I said. "The Arctic is very, very strange and sad. And toxic."

Robin let out an uncomfortable laugh. And Mr. Hoser didn't seem to appreciate this. "I wish all my students could engage themselves at this level with their assignments."

"Thank you," I said.

Then an office aide walked into my classroom and handed Mr. Hoser a note.

"Bessica," he said. "It looks like Principal Tidge wants to see you."

"Really?" I asked.

I searched my brain for reasons why this would be. But nothing came to mind.

"Maybe she wants to wish you good luck for the game," Mr. Hoser said.

"Maybe," I said. But I thought she could have accomplished that by sending me a polite note.

"Should I leave my things?" I asked.

"Maybe you should take them," Mr. Hoser said. "You don't know how long you'll be."

But that seemed like a terrible thing to say, because if Principal Tidge was really interested in wishing me good luck, that would take about two minutes.

"Should I leave my collage?" I asked. I tried to flatten its corners one last time.

"Yes!" Mr. Hoser said. "I'll hang it up along with the others."

When I got out into the hallway, I was surprised to see Cameron Bon Qui Qui. She hurried up to me. "You need to visit the row."

My mouth dropped open. Because the row was where

all the alt kids who were too dangerous to mingle with other kids hung out. I didn't belong there.

"I'm going to see Principal Tidge," I explained.

Cameron Bon Qui Qui looked nervous. "The note is fake. You're wanted on the row."

"Is this about Nadia?" I asked. Because I thought Nadia, who was the hardest hard-core alt person at my school (she wore a dog collar and had almost become my friend until she attacked a vending machine), was still suspended.

"This has nothing to do with Nadia. This is about your destiny," Cameron Bon Qui Qui said. "Now go!"

And the way she said that made me follow her directions. I rushed down the empty hallways until I had one turn left before the row. The lights flickered overhead, making the hallway dim. The row was a scary place for a normal person.

But then I turned the corner and I saw a bunch of my friends.

"We only have a few minutes," Annabelle explained.

"It's really good to see you guys!" I'd missed them at lunch because I'd had to meet my mom in the principal's office so she could check out my costume. And then we'd walked to the football field with Mrs. Batts so my mom knew exactly where I needed to be dropped off.

"We're worried about you," Lola said.

Oh, that was so sweet. "Thanks," I said.

"Are you going to wear a mask?" Macy asked me.

"Just my mascot head," I said.

"Your bear head might not be enough," Lola said.

"What if getting facebombed involves a stapler?" Jasper said.

Ooh. I hadn't realized that Jasper and I were close enough friends that he would skip class and meet me on the row and give me combat advice.

"You should bring a defensive object," Jasper said. "You need to arrive armed."

My eyes were huge. "I can't do that!"

That was when Jasper slapped the wall and I stared at him. "There is something nobody has told you yet about T.J."

Oh no. Based on the stories I'd heard so far, I was surprised that T.J. wasn't already in prison.

"He doesn't play fair," Jasper said.

"I know that," I said.

"No," Jasper said. "He's probably already got twenty-seven different plans for how he's going to facebomb you at the game. He's a planner. You can't go into this situation unaware."

"I'm totally aware," I said.

Jasper breathed very dramatically and pointed his finger right in my face. Annabelle bit her lower lip.

"I know how to facebomb somebody," Jasper said. "That's why I'm here. I'm going to teach you."

"Wow," I said. I was lucky to know people this generous. Though out of the corner of my eye I did see Annabelle frown a little.

"The best defense is a strong offense," Jasper said.

"That's why we're all here," Lola said.

Because I had zero idea what facebombing meant, these were magical words. "This is so fantastic," I said.

We heard the sound of a classroom door shut and Jasper jumped. "Uh-oh. I've got to go." He handed me a little slip of paper. "This is my number. Call me. I'm great at explaining battle plans over the phone."

Then Jasper raced off and Annabelle started breathing funny.

"Do you want to come over to my house when I call him and listen on the other end of the phone?" I asked.

Annabelle looked disgusted.

"What are you talking about? You can't call Jasper," Annabelle said.

Then Dee and Macy and Lola all nodded.

"Sisters before misters," Macy said.

"I didn't ask for his phone number," I said.

"But you have it," Annabelle said.

I held it up and Annabelle snatched it. Then she put

it in her mouth and chewed it. After she swallowed she said, "I've got to get back to class."

She hurried off very fast.

"You couldn't have called him anyway," Lola said. "That would stink of betrayal."

"Yeah," Dee said.

"Totally," Macy added.

"Okay. But I need help," I said. "I don't have any battle plans."

Squeak. Squeak. Squeak.

"Somebody's coming," Lola said.

"Bye," Dee said.

"See you," Macy said.

And I stood there while all my friends left me. Except for Lola. "Let's hide in the bathroom!"

Lola and I raced down the hallway to the bathroom. I needed help. I needed somebody to tell me what to do. We got to the bathroom and went into the second stall and shut the door.

"Bessica," Lola said. "Don't take what Annabelle said too personally."

But everything Annabelle said was personal.

"She's upset that Jasper likes you," Lola said.

"Jasper likes me?"

Lola nodded. "Lots of people get crushes on the mascot."

"Huh," I said. Because I did not know that.

"Out of respect for Annabelle, you should avoid all Jasper contact or the three of you might end up in a terrible crush triangle."

"What's that?"

Lola took a breath. "That's where one person likes one person and that person likes another person and so the first person hates the third."

"I would never hate Annabelle," I said.

"Right. But if you talk to Jasper, she'll hate you. That's how crush triangles operate."

My mind flashed to Willy and Grandma and Alma. Without even knowing it, by trying to turn Alma into a third wolf, I'd put those three in a crush triangle. I wondered who would end up hating who.

"You look very panicked. I didn't mean to scare you," Lola said. "I think you can avoid the crush triangle."

"I have so many problems," I mumbled.

"That's okay," Lola said. "I like complicated people."

I felt like crying. Right there in the bathroom, holding my bogus principal's note.

"You look sad," Lola said.

I kept quiet and swallowed several times. "What if something terrible happens to me at the game?"

"You'll live through it," Lola said.

"But what if something happens and I look stupid?" I said. Getting facebombed would probably be very humiliating.

"You'll live through that too," Lola said. "A lot of people think you're funny and cool. That's why you got half the votes."

But saying it that way made me think of the other half of the votes. Lola let out a big breath. "When I moved to this school two years ago, some people liked me and some people didn't."

I could really relate to what Lola was saying.

"And I wasn't very smart. Because I got all hung up on making the people who didn't like me like me. And I wasted a ton of time."

"Yeah," I said.

"You aren't hearing me," Lola said. "Don't worry about what other people think. Do what you want."

But I wasn't even sure what I wanted anymore.

"I want Sylvie to forgive me," I said.

"Have you told her that?" Lola asked.

I shook my head.

"You should," Lola said.

I nodded.

"Do you feel any better?" Lola asked.

"Lola," I said. "If you were me, would you try to face-bomb T.J. before he facebombed you?"

Lola shook her head. "I could never facebomb anybody. I think that's sort of barbaric."

"Yeah." Even though I had no idea what it meant to facebomb anybody, I said, "I totally think you're right."

CHAPTER

My mom and my grandma helped me get situated in my grizzly bear costume in the girls' locker room.

"You look so fierce," Grandma said.

"Should I start with my head on or off?" I asked.

Having my own head stuck in the bear head wasn't the most pleasant thing ever. Because my eyes had to look out of these wire mesh areas. And the air grew a little thick inside there and made my head sweat.

"I think you start with the head on," Grandma said. "And when you need to take it off, remember to set it on a chair."

"I knew that!" I said.

My mom took a whole bunch of pictures of me. "Growl at me," she encouraged. "Swing your paws."

I did not feel like doing these things on command. Because a bear wouldn't.

I was sort of upset that my mom was acting like this, because some of the cheerleaders were getting ready with me, and their moms weren't here taking pictures of them.

"Good luck, Bessica," one of the cheerleaders said.

"Thanks," I said.

And then all the cheerleaders drifted to a different area of the locker room, where they began to practice hand drills. *Smack. Snap. Slap. Smack. Snap. Slap.*

"Bessica," my mom said, trying to get my attention.

"Maybe I should have learned some hand drills," I said. Because watching other people do those made me realize that they looked cool.

"Seems hard to pull off with your fur mitts," Grandma said.

I looked at my furry hands. She was right.

"Think of all the wild bears we saw at Bear Galaxy," my mom encouraged me. "Channel them."

I took my head off and held it. "Those bears didn't act wild at all. They were miserable."

"They did look a little forlorn," Grandma said. "Captivity will do that to apex predators. You can't even keep a great white shark alive in captivity. They always, always, always die."

My mom and I stared at Grandma when she said that.

"That's terrible," I said.

"Well, aquariums usually shorten marine life by decades," Grandma said. "Those places are basically marine mortuaries."

"Let's not talk about this before Bessica's big game. Let's pump her up," my mom said.

Grandma agreed. "O fierce one," Grandma said, giving me a hug. "Get out there and dazzle them. And don't forget your prop bag."

I glanced at the bench where I'd set my prop bag. It contained my jump rope, two emergency pom-poms that I hoped I'd never have to use, and a bunch of cheers I'd printed out. "I hope I'm loud enough."

"Willy and I could hear your cheers from the Winnebago. You're plenty loud," Grandma said.

I watched as the cheerleaders left the locker room. "We're going out to the field," the captain said. "Pregame show starts soon. You'll want to be there for that."

"Right," I said.

After they left, the room felt very quiet and echoey.

"Is it time?" I asked. "Or should I wait?"

"I think it's time," my mom said.

Walking across the parking lot toward the football field was a very nervous experience.

"I'm getting my hind paws dirty," I said. "I think I stepped in a puddle."

"We'll wash them later," my mom said.

The stadium was filled with people. And all the football players, from both schools, were out on the field running around.

"Oh," Grandma said, pointing to a fuzzy orange person. "Is that T.J. the Tiger?"

It made me sort of sick that Grandma would point him out like that to me. Because it was T.J. the Tiger.

"I hate that guy," I said.

"Bessica," my mom said. "*Hate* is a strong word."

"It really is," I said.

I stopped walking and stood and looked at everything. It was a late-afternoon game, and there were rows and rows of cheering fans. The playing field looked very green and the goalposts looked very straight. And the hash marks appeared freshly chalked onto the field.

During PE, I had only been allowed to practice on the field one time. And I really hadn't done that much. I'd just sort of run from one end zone to the other and then done some stretching. Now that the field was covered with players, it seemed different.

"Bessica!" somebody called. I started looking around.

I really hoped it was Sylvie. But it wasn't. It was Vicki Docker.

"Wow," I said. "You came to my game?" She must have liked me a whole lot more than I'd realized. Because it was a Friday and she probably had cool high school things to do.

"I was driving past on my way to the mall and I saw all the cars!" Vicki said. "I wanted to stop and wish you luck."

That made more sense.

"I hope you let your inner cheer beast shine!" Vicki said.

"Yeah," I said.

But it seemed like in order to let my inner cheer beast shine, I would have to attack T.J. I didn't know what to do.

"Good luck!" Vicki said as she ran off the field. "And put your head on." I put my head on and watched Vicki through my mesh eye slots as she made her way to her car. A boy was waiting in the driver's seat. Maybe she was on a date. It made me wonder if I would ever go on a date. I thought of Noll and Bianca. Everything felt so up in the air.

And then it happened. I thought I was going to have all this time to stretch and prepare and get ready for the game. But I was wrong. One minute I was wondering about my gorgeous neighbor, Noll Beck. And the next I saw T.J. standing right in front of me. He had his head on. I had my head on. And the smack talking began.

"Hey," I said. "Stay on your own side."

But T.J. didn't answer me with words. He pulled a flyswatter out and started smacking me with it.

"Stop that," I said. Because I thought that it would have made sense to swat me if I was a fly or a bee or a mosquito mascot. But I was a bear.

"Wimpy bear!" T.J. yelled. "Wimpy bear!"

And that was when I heard people starting to laugh. And they weren't really laughing at anything I was doing. They were laughing because I was getting slapped with a flyswatter, and that felt terrible.

"Seriously," I said to T.J. "Get back on your own turf."

But instead of doing that, he slapped me with the flyswatter right on my face. I was in shock. Was he face-bombing me? I didn't know. Instead of attacking him, I thought of something else. I reached in my prop bag and pulled out my jump rope. T.J. stood back a little bit and I did a few tricks. I swung the rope like a helicopter and then jumped through it. And I jump-roped over to the football coaches and then I stopped and put my paws out and they high-fived me. And then I jump-roped over to the players.

And instead of acting afraid of them because they were popular football players, I started patting them on their backs in a supportive way. I even swatted a few more on the butt. And when that happened, the crowd laughed. And when they did that, I held my pawed hand up to my ear to see if the crowd would laugh louder and they did. So I put my paw up to my other ear. And then I slapped a coach on the butt. Not in a mean way.

Laugh. Laugh. Laugh.

Things felt really great. It was as if I was born to be a mascot. I felt brave and happy and bearlike.

But this wasn't enough. I wanted people to laugh harder. Plus, I needed to stop playing with the team. Once the game started, I wasn't allowed to bother them. So I headed back toward the stands. With my bear mascot head on, it was really hard to keep an eye out for T.J., because all I could see was the area directly in front of my mesh eyeholes. And that area jostled when I ran.

While I was running toward the crowd, my world jostling, something very unfortunate happened to me and my bear head. I tripped. Big-time. And before I had time to react or figure out if T.J. and his mean tricks were behind my stumble, my head fell off. Because gravity was basically the only thing holding it on. The crowd exploded in laughter. Which wasn't how I wanted things to happen. I wanted to lead them in laughter. I didn't want them to laugh at me because I looked like a stupid person. I stood up as fast as I could. T.J. wasn't going to kick my butt this easily. And that was when I realized that T.J. wasn't anywhere around me. I'd tripped over a divot in the grass. Oops. I needed to be on the lookout for uneven turf.

I dusted myself off in a dramatic fashion and the crowd kept laughing. While my head was off I decided it would be a good time to do some head-off cheers. So I did.

"Roll it! Shake it! Beat it up and bake it!" I rolled my arms energetically and shook my hips and wiggled my butt. "Honey and sugar, you're gonna lose. Honey and sugar, eat our boos!" I lifted my paw hand to my ear and the crowd erupted in boos. They booed so loudly that it made the hair on my arms stand up.

Being a mascot felt pretty great. It was just like I'd dreamed it. Even falling on my face hadn't ruined things. That was the cool thing about being a mascot. If you did something clumsy or stupid, people assumed you meant to do it. "Roll it! Shake it!" Finally, I felt popular. At last, Bessica Lefter had arrived.

But then everything changed. Out of the corner of my eye, I spotted Grandma. She stood next to Willy, waving. I waved back. And I saw my dad filming me. And I suddenly had the desire to be Flip-cammed with Grandma. So I put my bear head back on and ran up to her. She put her arm around me.

"I'm so proud of you! Your performance is surpassing my wildest dreams," Grandma said.

I felt the exact same way. My performance was surpassing *my* wildest dreams too. Then I ran back to the field. But when I did, I stumbled. And I crashed in a sliding way onto the grass. I heard somebody from the bleachers yell, "The bear fell down again. He's hilarious!"

I wanted to pull my head off so he could see I wasn't a he. But I didn't. I crawled onto my knees and was about to get up when I heard somebody laughing right next to me.

"Time to hibernate!" T.J. yelled.

I felt myself getting smacked with the flyswatter again. He was getting the floppy plastic part really close to my mesh eye area, and I didn't like that.

"Stop it!" I said.

"I'm a tiger. I don't stop. I slaughter." T.J. roared like a crazy maniac and swished his tail and it made the hair on my arms stand up—in a bad way.

As he stood over me, laughing and being rude, I decided to retaliate. I reached up and yanked on his tail. But it didn't come off like I'd hoped. I tugged harder, but instead of the tail breaking off, T.J. fell on top of me.

"Knock it off," T.J. said.

But I didn't knock it off. Because in my bear suit I didn't feel scared or worried. I felt powerful and brave. I yanked on his tail again. This time I pulled on it so hard that I sprang to my feet. I needed to bring it. Because I was a mascot. And mascots didn't give up. Mascots dialed up their mojo until they won. I quickly glanced at the field. I'd lost track of both the score and who had possession of the ball. Uh-oh. But I didn't let that stop me from cheering. I took my head off and set it on an empty seat.

"I want a touchdown! I want a trout! If you get in my way, I'll rip your guts out!" And then I growled ferociously while still holding T.J.'s tail.

"Your team isn't even close to the end zone. You're nuts," T.J. said. "And give me my tail back."

But I didn't. "What do we eat? What do we eat? Tiger meat! Tiger meat! How do we like it? How do we like it? Raw! Raw! Raw!"

Yank. Yank. Yank.

Even though he tried very hard to get away, I wouldn't let him. I held his tail hard. Then I heard myself roar the biggest roar and then I sank my teeth into the tiger's unbreakable tail.

"She's biting me!" T.J. yelled. "That's not allowed."

"Bessica!" a voice cried that sounded a lot like my mom's. "Don't bite the other mascot."

Hearing my mom yell at me to stop biting the other mascot made me reconsider my level of ferociousness, so I released T.J.'s tail from my teeth.

"Get ready. I'm taking you down," T.J. said.

I knew what was coming. I stood wide in my bear stance and prepared to be facebombed. But he walked off. Where was he going? He was heading toward Grandma and Willy. No! Was he going to facebomb Grandma?

I ran after him. "Stay away from my grandma," I yelled.

But then T.J. started running full speed toward my grandma. And when he got right next to her he made a thumbs-down sign.

I couldn't believe it.

"Stop making rude hand gestures at my grandma!" I shouted.

But he didn't stop. He made thumbs-down signs with both hands. I grabbed him by his tail again and pulled him away from Grandma.

"Bessica, you can't yank on his costume," a voice that sounded a lot like my dad said.

"Yes I can!" I said.

T.J. was a lot stronger than I was. He jerked himself free. He narrowed his eyes and huffed. Then he licked his lips. "Prepare to get facebombed."

But I was so worked up that I didn't even feel any fear. I narrowed my eyes and huffed. Then I licked my lips and I thought of the most threatening thing I could say. "Oh yeah! Prepare to get narwhaled!"

Then I closed my eyes and charged him. The sound that

escaped him as I tackled him reminded me of a deflating balloon. Once we were both on the ground, I decided to declare a total victory by sitting on him. Which I did, while yelling, "I declare a total victory!"

Then all the people parted and I looked up and saw Principal Tidge. "Off the field!" she said.

T.J.'s tiger head had fallen off and rolled away from his body. I wasn't sure if she was talking to me or T.J. Neither one of us moved an inch.

"Both of you!" Principal Tidge said.

"You're toast," he whispered to me as we got off the ground.

"No. You're toast," I said.

"You aren't allowed to touch the other mascot," T.J. said.

"You touched me with a flyswatter," I said.

Then he bumped me. And I couldn't believe that he'd do that. So I bumped him back. Then I felt him put his hand on my back and he shoved me. And I was shocked! Because a boy shouldn't shove a girl ever, even if he is dressed like a tiger. So I turned around and told him that.

"You are a terrible person!" I said. "Stop shoving girls!"

"I'm not shoving girls," he said. "I'm shoving you."

By this time, coaches from both teams had arrived and Principal Tidge got between us. And then Mom and Dad and Grandma and Willy were there.

"This is the height of unsportsmanlike conduct," said the other coach.

"It's flagrant," said our home team coach, whose name I'd forgotten but whose height was staggering.

"I need them both off the field!" a referee said.

"Absolutely," Principal Tidge said. "Bessica needs to go home."

I scanned the crowd for my friends. I hadn't even gotten a chance to say hello to them.

"Bessica!" Lola yelled. I saw her waving. She was with Annabelle, Macy, and Dee. To demonstrate team spirit, they had their faces painted with thick purple lines. And then Jasper rushed up too. But his face wasn't painted.

"I'll call or text you!" Annabelle cried.

"Way to block the facebomb!" Jasper yelled.

But then Principal Tidge said something that distracted me from my friends. "Our school has a zero violence policy. Even for mascots. Expect a phone call about disciplinary action."

I hung my head. The coaches and referee drifted back to the playing field.

"And T.J.," Principal Tidge said. "You've really pushed things to the limit this time."

"What did I do?" T.J. said. "She's crazy and I'm innocent."

"Don't insult my eyesight," Principal Tidge said. "I saw everything."

Then Principal Tidge hauled T.J. into the school and said they were going to call his principal and parents. I stood with Mom, Dad, Grandma, and Willy while my principal and mascot enemy walked into the building.

"That didn't go so hot," I said.

"Bessica," my mom said. "What were you thinking? You can't bite the other mascot."

"He was a terror!" Grandma said. "Very unsportsman-like conduct indeed."

"Let's go home," Dad said. "Too bad we're going to miss the game."

"I feel sort of rotten," I said.

"You should," my mom said. "You just got ejected."

And the way my mom said that word made me feel awful.

"I didn't mean to get ejected," I said.

"You were off to such a good start," Grandma said. "But once he began assaulting you with a flyswatter, things really started to nosedive."

"That's true," I said.

"Let's not relive it," my mom said as we walked to the car. "We're going to have to wait for Principal Tidge to call."

"Do you think I'll get suspended from my next game?"

"They have a second mascot, Bessica," my mom said,

sounding very frustrated. "I wouldn't be surprised if they revoked your mascot status after this."

"Really?" I asked. "You mean I wouldn't be a mascot at all anymore?" I couldn't imagine what it would feel like to be in sixth grade and not be a mascot.

"That probably won't happen," my dad said.

"Don't set her up for disappointment, Buck," my mom said. "Anything could happen. Her mascot future could be over like that." My mom snapped her fingers to communicate how quickly I could lose my mascot position.

Snap!

We drove in silence for a long time.

"I don't know what the rest of you thought, but that tiger kid looked like a complete dweeb," Willy said.

"Yeah," I mumbled.

My mother let out a big, disappointed breath. "That might be true, but biting dweebs is not allowed."

"I only bit his tail," I explained. "It was all stuffing."

"Bessica," my mother said in a stern voice. "A bite is a bite."

"Your mom's right. You probably won't get off scot-free," my dad said.

"Let's listen to the radio," Grandma said.

And a song about a roller coaster came on. And that felt appropriate. Because I felt like I was riding one of those. And I knew right where it was headed.

The principal's office.

CHAPTER

All day Saturday I sat in my room and stared at Bianca. She didn't do much. She slept. She ate. She licked up water beads from her plastic tree. The crickets were more interesting. It felt like I was watching an adventure movie as the powdered bugs tried to figure out ways to escape. They tried crawling up the aquarium's slippery glass walls or squeezing under the cage's Astroturf-lined bottom. They knew they were about to become lizard food. And they wanted to find a better life.

I'd dropped these crickets inside the cage two days ago. They didn't have much longer. Poor crickets. I didn't know if it was because I was waiting for my punishment or if it was because I'd recently been trapped in a cafeteria, but I could relate to these bugs on a very deep level. I wanted to save them.

I hurried to the kitchen to get some Tupperware.

"You look much more cheerful," Grandma said. She and Willy were flipping through a book together at the kitchen table.

"Where's the lid for this?" I asked, holding up a big plastic rectangle.

"Check the dishwasher," Grandma said.

I found it. I also grabbed some rubber gloves. And paper towels.

"Cleaning?" Grandma asked.

"Kind of," I said as I headed back to my room.

My heart raced as I gloved my hands and stuck them in Bianca's cage. I didn't normally wear gloves when I put my hands in the cage. But touching live crickets seemed risky. "Stupid crickets," I said. Because they kept jumping away from my hands.

Knock. Knock. Knock.

Grandma opened the door. "Sylvie's here." Then she saw what I was doing and frowned. "What are you doing to that poor lizard?"

"Nothing," I said. I was so excited that Sylvie was here. "I'm liberating the crickets before they die."

"Didn't we just buy those crickets?" Grandma asked.

I didn't answer. I looked behind Grandma and saw Sylvie's head. I waved.

"I'll leave you two alone to talk," Grandma said.

"Thank you so much for coming over to visit me," I said. I wanted to rush up and give Sylvie a hug. But I also wanted her to do something to signal it was okay for me to rush her.

"I heard about your game ejection," Sylvie said.

I was sort of sad to hear that Sylvie hadn't been at my game and had only heard about it.

"T.J. was making rude hand gestures at Grandma. I had to do something," I said.

"Rumor is you completely throttled him," Sylvie said.

We were still separated by the length of my room.

"I'm a bear mascot," I said. "So I went a little 'bear' on him."

Sylvie smiled at that.

"When he finally showed up at my birthday party he was a complete nightmare," Sylvie said.

I nodded enthusiastically. "That's why I acted so weird and accidentally crashed into your cake," I explained. "I was trying to get out of there."

Sylvie walked a few steps closer to me. Then she sat on my bed. "Why didn't you tell me that?"

I sat down next to her. "I don't know. I guess I didn't want anybody to think I was a wimpy mascot."

"Well, nobody thinks that now," Sylvie said. "Our bee mascot, Kirby, is terrified to cheer against you."

I looked up and made a sympathetic face. "Oh, tell her not to be. I only attack jerks who personally threaten me or insult my grandma."

Sylvie smiled huge when I said that. "You are so funny."

"You're so funny too."

Knock. Knock. Knock.

"Would anybody inside this room care for pie?" Grandma asked.

"Sure," I said.

"Weren't you going to liberate the crickets?" Sylvie asked.

"I guess. But I'd just have to buy more."

"Sort this out and join Willy and me and Alma and Pete at your leisure."

"Pete?" I asked. I didn't like that a strange man was in my house and I didn't know about it.

"Alma's long-distance boyfriend," Grandma said.

"What?" I asked.

"Alma's boyfriend," Grandma said again. "Pete from Florida."

Then I heard a bizarre laugh that sounded like a duck. "Is that *him*?" I asked.

"Yes," Grandma said. "He's very gregarious."

"Poor Alma," I said. Not only did her boyfriend live very far away, but he also had a terrible laugh.

Then Grandma left. And I asked Sylvie a very important question. "What do you call a triangle when you add a corner to it?"

"A square."

I gasped. I'd created a terrible square crush between Grandma, Willy, Alma, and Florida Pete. Except maybe it wasn't terrible.

"I tried to break up Willy and Grandma," I explained.

"Again?" Sylvie asked. "You need to accept that he's your grandma's permanent boyfriend."

Those were very sad words. Very sad indeed.

Sylvie reached into her bag and pulled out her nose hair trimmer. "I want to give this back to you. Your present really hurt my feelings."

I took the trimmer and stared at its tiny round blade. "It was a terrible gift," I said. "I don't know what I was thinking. I'm sorry."

Then we were both quiet. I set the trimmer down and took off my plastic yellow gloves and tossed them next to Bianca's cage. Then I realized that Sylvie didn't know that this was Noll Beck's lizard and that he and his girlfriend had broken up. So I rushed to tell her this. "I have the craziest story to tell you about gorgeous Noll Beck!"

But Sylvie looked at me like she already knew. "I heard. But don't worry. It sounds like his surgery was very minor."

"What?" I asked. "Who got surgery?"

"Noll Beck. While riding, he was thrown and had his shoulder dislocated. He had to have surgery."

I felt awful. My possible future boyfriend had been hospitalized and I'd had no idea.

"When did this happen?" I asked.

"Yesterday."

At the exact same time I was fending off T.J., gorgeous Noll Beck was getting trampled by a horse.

"I hate horses," I said.

"I think he was messing around and got thrown off a cow," Sylvie said.

"I hate cows even more!"

Sylvie shook her head. "No you don't. You eat hamburgers more than anybody I know."

And it felt so good to be talking to a friend who knew so much about me.

"This means we're friends again, right?" I asked.

"You need to watch the tone in your texts," Sylvie said.

"Yeah. I didn't realize how easy it is to send mean texts until I fired off a bunch to you."

"Mine were sort of rude too, and I apologize for that."

I swung my arm over Sylvie's shoulder and gave her a hug.

"What happens next?" Sylvie asked.

"I'm waiting to learn about my punishment."

"That's so harsh."

"I just hope I get to keep being the mascot."

"You think they'd take that away from you?"

"They might," I said. "In the worst-case scenario."

Sylvie and I both stared at Bianca's cage. I felt bad that we'd run out of things to talk about.

"I should probably get going," Sylvie said.

"Why?" Because I still had a bunch of free time.

"I'm meeting Malory at the mall," Sylvie said.

I didn't really enjoy hearing about Sylvie's other friends. "Okay. Have fun."

"Can't you be a little happy for me? I've been trying hard to make new friends."

"But I'm your friend," I said. "I've been your friend the longest and I'll always be your friend. Forever."

Sylvie put her arm around me. "I know. It's like we're sisters."

And when Sylvie said that, I had a hard time not crying. Because that was the exact way I felt about her. We weren't just two random people who met in grade school and started riding our bicycles together. We were like family.

"I hope you have a good time at the mall," I said.

"Will you call and tell me about your punishment as soon as you find out?"

"Absolutely," I said.

Then Sylvie pulled away from me and stood up.

"I wonder how much longer you'll have to keep his lizard. Postsurgery, I bet he can't really even lift stuff, let alone take care of a reptile."

"I'll take care of Bianca as long as I need to," I said.

A white cricket darted across Sylvie's foot and she screamed. "They escape?"

"All the time," I said.

"You must really truly like Noll Beck."

"Yeah," I said. "I really truly do."

CHAPTER

19

We got the call on Monday that my disciplinary action was more severe than anybody had suspected. My principal was very disappointed in me. So was my mom. And my dad. And Grandma. I didn't really care what Willy thought. That night at dinner it was the first thing that came up.

"Never in a million years did I think that you would face disciplinary action in middle school!" my mom said.

"Me either," I said.

But I also had never imagined a situation where a tiger mascot would insult Grandma at a football game in front of two hundred people.

We sat at the dinner table and tried to eat chicken and dumplings. I wasn't sure my mom had made them properly. Everything looked gray. Even the carrots.

"That other kid got suspended," my dad said.

"Yeah," I said, trying to defend myself a little bit.

"The only reason that happened was because they found a cooler he'd brought filled with balloons that were stuffed with shaving cream, and his school has a strict policy against balloons," my mom said. "It's not like he *bit* Bessica."

"He shoved me," I said.

"Lots of kids face disciplinary action and go on to live respectable and wonderful lives," Grandma said as she took a big, juicy bite of a dumpling.

"I got suspended once," Willy said.

"Ooh. What did you do?" I asked, because having my family talk about Willy's suspension would be easier on me than having my family talk about my problems.

"I brought firecrackers to school and lit them during class," Willy said.

"Whoa!" I said. "That's hard-core. At my school, fireworks are considered weapons."

"Okay," my mom said, interrupting. "Let's not glorify delinquency. Let's focus on preparing Bessica for the punishment panel."

"It's not called that," I said. When Principal Tidge called

my house, she had informed my mom that on Thursday I would have to go before a peer review panel to determine my punishment. And a peer review panel was exactly that. A group of kids from my middle school who would determine how much trouble I was actually in.

"According to Principal Tidge, no parents are present during the review. Bessica gives a speech. Then the students call witnesses."

"Ooh," I said. "There are a lot of those."

"That's not necessarily a good thing," my mom said.

I spooned a dumpling into my mouth.

"What's your defense?" my dad asked.

I shrugged and chewed my dumpling.

"They're going to want to know why you bit the tiger," my dad said. "Your punishment hinges on your answer."

I swallowed. "I wanted to humiliate him before he could humiliate me."

My mother groaned. "You need to be honest and sympathetic at the same time."

That sounded hard.

"Your mom's right," my dad said. "You're going to need a better answer."

"Let's not pressure her too much," Grandma said. "I'm sure when the time comes, Bessica will have a perfectly good answer for her punishment panel."

I frowned. "It's not called that, Grandma."

* * *

As I waited to face the peer review panel, the days dragged on and nothing at school felt normal. Not riding the bus. Not going to class. Not talking to my friends. Not eating lunch. Not even sitting alone and thinking. It was a very stressful time.

The night before the peer review I couldn't get to sleep. Because I realized that more than anything, I wanted to keep being the mascot. My mother drove me to school and walked me to the principal's office.

"I'll wait out here," she said.

"But what if it takes over an hour?" I asked.

"I'll wait." She sat down in a chair next to Mrs. Batts's desk.

"Mom," I said, before I went into Principal Tidge's office. "I am sorry I did this."

My mom looked on the verge of tears. "I know you are." She wiped her eyes. "I just don't remember middle school being this hard, Bessica. Look around. You should be enjoying yourself."

I did not look around. When my mom said crazy things like that, it made it a lot harder for me to connect with her.

"Wait!" Mrs. Batts said. "The peer review is taking place in room 211."

"It is?" I asked.

Mrs. Batts led me quickly by the shoulder to the room. She walked me in. It was terrible. "Why are so many people here?" I asked.

"Well," Mrs. Batts said. "There are eight students on the peer review panel. And then there are witnesses who the panel has asked to question. And then a couple of people asked to come to speak on your behalf."

I searched the crowd. I didn't recognize anybody who'd want to be here on my behalf. Then Duke the eagle walked in the room and he was with Pierre the spud and I recognized them right away because they were dressed like mascots. They waved to me.

"Are they in trouble too?" I asked.

Mrs. Batts rubbed my arm sympathetically. "No, just you."

The chairs were arranged in a semicircle. And there was an empty chair in front of them.

"That's where you sit," Principal Tidge said. She was dressed in an unfriendly black skirt and a stiff gray top.

I took my seat and stared out at my peers. They were all people I knew. Ooh. Some looked sympathetic. But some did not. I went through the names in my head and decided who I thought would be on my side.

Robin Lord: Liked me okay.
Cameron Bon Qui Qui: Mostly did not like me.

Jasper Finch: Liked me quite a bit.

Dolan the Puker: Not sure. Jealous that I was voted mascot.

Blake Bradshaw: Enormous dweeb. Probably liked me.

Davis Pontiac: Locker above me. Liked me.

Dee Hsu: Loved me! My friend.

Raya Papas: Wild card.

"We all know why we're here," Principal Tidge said. "Before Bessica speaks, we have two guests who have asked to say a few words on her behalf."

Everybody stared at the eagle and the spud. Even I did.

"Duke and Pierre, could you please come to the front of the room?"

They looked so solemn as they walked to the whiteboard. Duke lost a couple of feathers and they floated in the air behind him. Then he took off his head and spoke.

"I'm Duke. The Flat Creek Bald Eagle." He bowed a little.

"I'm Pierre. The Powderhorn Spud." He waved.

"I'd actually like to begin by asking Pierre a question," Duke said. "How many times have you cheered against T.J. the Tiger?"

"Four times," Pierre said.

I sort of wished he wasn't in his spud costume, because

he looked funny, almost like a joke. And I wasn't sure that I wanted people who were speaking in my defense to look like jokes.

"How would you characterize T.J. as a mascot?" Duke asked. He lifted his feathered arm up in a thoughtful way.

"He's rotten. Totally, completely, absolutely rotten."

I looked out at the panel. Robin nodded a little bit. That was a great sign!

"Care to share any stories?" Duke asked.

Pierre cleared his throat. "I had prepared a few stories about all the unspeakable acts I've seen T.J. perpetrate against other mascots, but looking at Bessica sitting on that chair of judgment, I feel compelled to say something else."

I squirmed a little. I didn't like to think of myself as being seated in a chair of judgment.

"How many of you have ever dressed up like a potato?" Pierre asked.

Nobody raised their hand. Except for Pierre.

"An eagle? A cougar? A falcon? A bear?" Pierre continued.

I raised my hand.

"How many of you have put on a costume and stood outside in the elements and risked being teased and mocked, and in the face of those risks, who has tried to rally a crowd's team spirit?"

Pierre paced in front of the whiteboard while he spoke. Everybody seemed fascinated by him. Even I was.

"What mascots do is hard work. We strive. We risk. We offer ourselves up in front of everybody and sacrifice our own dignity for laughter and cheers."

I had not thought of myself that way.

"Bessica Lefter is a hero. Because in addition to striving and risking for her team, she also stood up to a well-known bully. She didn't bite T.J. out of anger. She bit that tiger out of fear."

I nodded a bunch when Pierre said this.

"I know who Bessica Lefter is. In a way, I feel like I am Bessica Lefter. And you and you and you. You are all Bessica Lefter."

Raya Papas looked disgusted when she was called Bessica Lefter.

"Bessica was just trying to do her best. Her first game cheering, and the opposing mascot brought a cooler filled with balloons stuffed with shaving cream? Maybe some of you aren't familiar with that tactic, but it's called facebombing. T.J. came out onto that field fully intending to facebomb Bessica when your team scored its first goal. She'd heard of this threat, but she went out there anyway. Don't punish her too harshly for what she did. She was standing up for her team. Her school. Remember, you too are Bessica Lefter. And you. And you. And you. Be lenient."

"I am not Bessica Lefter," Raya Papas said loudly.

"Thank you," Principal Tidge said. "I have one question for Bessica before we go any further."

This frightened me. Because just one question meant that there was probably just one right answer.

"Had T.J. threatened you prior to the game?" Principal Tidge leaned forward in her chair.

Her eyes were so powerful, they made my whole body feel hot and nervous. I looked above me at the light as it beamed down on me like the sun. Sweat formed at my hairline. One lone drop rolled down the side of my face all the way to my neck. But I knew the answer to this one. Why was I so worried?

"Yes," I said. "He did."

Principal Tidge leaned back in her chair. "Well, that changes things." She stood up. "Peer review, you are all dismissed. You won't be deciding Bessica's punishment. I will. This isn't a case of a mascot gone wrong. What we have here is a complex bullying situation."

"Really?" I asked. I had suspected we had a bullying situation, but I'd had no idea it was complex.

Everybody filed out of the room, and as Dee left she whispered, "You were going to get off light anyway."

I smiled.

But Principal Tidge wasn't smiling, so I stopped.

"Bessica, biting is barbaric."

"Yeah," I said, sounding a little ashamed.

"I'm sorry to hear about the facebomb situation, but what you did was wrong."

"I feel very bad about it," I said.

She walked over to me and handed me a piece of paper. "Twenty hours," she said.

"Of what?" I asked, taking the paper.

"Fire safety training for grades kindergarten through three. I'm certain you'll be excellent."

"Okay," I said. I folded the paper and put it in my pocket. "My mom is outside. Do you need to talk to her?"

"That's a good idea."

I followed Principal Tidge into the hallway, and she asked me to wait there so she could talk to my mom. As I leaned against the wall I saw somebody I really didn't want to see: Alice Potgeiser. She looked so happy. She strutted right up to me, smiling, and handed me a slip of paper. "Here's my address. You can drop off the bear paws at your earliest convenience."

"Why would I give you my bear paws?"

Alice faked a sympathy frown. "I wrote a persuasive letter to the peer review asking them to suspend you from all further football games."

I couldn't believe that Alice had tried to get me suspended for the entire football season. She was evil!

"Take it," Alice said, thrusting the paper at me. "Your

mom will need to follow the map on the back. MapQuest always sends people the wrong way once they cross the bridge."

I shook my head. I didn't need a map to Alice Potgeiser's house. "Sorry to break your heart, but I'm still half mascot. I wasn't suspended."

Alice looked horrified. "That's impossible! My letter was very convincing. I outlined how you repeatedly mauled the opposing team's mascot and are unsafe to take the field!"

I held my finger up and wagged it a little to let her know that I disagreed with that assessment. "I didn't maul anybody. What we've got here is a complicated bullying situation."

My mom stepped into the hallway and interrupted my terrible conversation with Alice.

"That went so much better than I thought it would," my mom said.

Alice didn't wait around to hear any more. She flipped around. "Mauler," she mumbled as she huffed off.

My mom didn't really notice Alice's melodramatic exit. She walked up to me and gave me a big hug.

"I have to teach elementary school kids about fire safety for twenty hours," I said.

"Not in a row," my mom replied, releasing her grip on me.

As we walked to the car I realized that maybe my mom was right and I should be having more fun in middle school.

"I want to hang out with Sylvie again," I said.

"I know," my mom said.

"I need to call Lola," I said.

"Okay."

"Does this mean I won't be grounded?" I asked.

"Let me discuss it with your father," my mom said.

"It would be nice if I could invite Sylvie and Lola over," I said. "And maybe also the spud and eagle mascots."

"You want to invite boys over?" my mom asked as she climbed into the car.

"I do," I said. "I'm mature enough to have boys as friends."

"Oh brother," my mom said.

"I promise I'll never bite another mascot ever again," I said.

"You shouldn't have to make that promise. That should be basic operating procedure."

"Yeah." Even though I was a very dedicated mascot bear, I knew my mom was right.

CHAPTER

I was surprised that Sylvie, Lola, Duke, and Pierre got along in my living room as well as they did. It was as if we were all meant to be friends.

"Thanks again for coming over and helping me sort through my fire safety materials," I said.

"After reading this pamphlet, I'll never look at an electrical socket the same way again," Duke said.

Not wearing his eagle outfit and not having a nose zit, he looked a lot cuter than he had when I first met him. But even though Duke was cute, I didn't *like him* like him. Because I had already given my heart to the gorgeous and tragically cow-injured Noll Beck. Maybe Duke could become Sylvie's boyfriend. Ooh!

"You're going to scare all the kids into never touching a lamp if you tell them this story," Lola said, pointing to a different pamphlet that outlined the dangers of putting flammable materials near heat sources and lightbulbs.

"Let's face it," I said. "My punishment is sort of a bummer."

"You can still have fun with it," Sylvie said. "Do you get to go dressed as a bear?"

"I think that's the idea," I said.

"Be careful," Pierre said. "Your costume is extremely flammable."

I sighed. I didn't need to be that careful. The fire marshal was going to be standing right next to me.

"Basically, I only need to teach the kids four things," I explained. I stood on my couch so I could be higher than everybody else while I delivered my message. "Remind your parents to change the batteries in your smoke alarm once a year. Clean your clothes dryer vent. Fireworks have the potential to blow off your fingers and cause forest fires. Make sure you know two ways to escape your house if it bursts into flames."

"You're going to make people cry," Lola said.

"Maybe," I said as I stepped off the couch. "But I'll be

very calm when I talk. And I'll be dressed like a bear. And everything I'm telling them is excellent information."

"How are things going in there?" my mom asked.

"Great," I said.

But we all looked pretty gloomy.

"Do you want to show your friends how to feed the lizard?" my mom asked. "Grandma just bought new crickets."

"That won't work," I said. "I have to feed the crickets essential vitamins first. And that takes at least one day."

Everybody looked disappointed to learn this, especially Duke.

"Okay," I said. "Just this once we can do it without gut loading the crickets first."

So we all walked in a line straight to my bedroom.

"This is so disgusting," Lola said. "I love it!"

I opened a plastic bag and poured a little bit of calcium powder inside. Then I shook it like mad. "It fortifies Bianca's bones," I explained.

"How many crickets are in there?" Pierre asked.

"We buy them by the dozen," I said.

My friends looked horrified. Then I opened Bianca's cage and dumped the white crickets inside.

"I've never seen one animal eat another animal," Pierre said.

"Even on television?" Sylvie asked.

Pierre didn't have time to answer. Because Bianca leaped from her plastic tree and landed on the cage's bottom and snapped up a cricket in one quick bite.

Everybody screamed.

"Look! Duke said. "Its legs are still moving. It's not dead yet."

But then Bianca swallowed the rest of the bug whole.

"It's dead now," I said.

Hanging out watching Noll Beck's lizard eat bugs with my friends was a pretty good way to spend the day. "Noll is so lucky to have you as a neighbor," Lola said. "Because I could never do that."

"That thing looks like a dinosaur," Pierre said.

"No it doesn't," Lola said.

"If that thing doesn't look like a dinosaur, then what does it look like?" Pierre asked.

"A lizard," Lola said.

I sensed a little friction between those two, but in a good way.

"I can't watch more crickets get snapped in two," Sylvie said. "What should we do next?"

"Ooh," I said. "I know. Have you guys ever seen a narwhal?"

Sylvie, Lola, Pierre, and Duke all just stared at me. "It's a whale with a nine-foot horn tooth. Willy bought me a DVD of one. And there's also polar bears. It's a little bloody."

After I liked the one he rented so much, he had bought a copy for me. It was a pretty nice thing to do.

"That sounds cool," Duke said.

"Let's watch it," Pierre said.

"How much blood?" Sylvie asked.

I put my arm around her. "There's only two blood-gushing scenes."

Lola kept staring at Bianca. "Have you sent Noll a picture of her lately?"

I shook my head.

"You should hold Bianca and I'll send him a picture of that. It's a good idea to send people you like your picture."

"Shhh," I said. I didn't want Pierre and Duke to know that I liked Noll.

"Isn't Noll Beck in high school?" Duke asked.

"We're just really good friends. I watch his lizard when he's out of town. And he does stuff for me."

"Like what?" Duke asked.

What did Noll Beck do for me?

"He's an awesome listener," I said. Because when I spoke he usually remembered what I said.

"Okay," Lola said. "I'm ready."

I reached into the aquarium and grabbed Bianca behind

the head so she couldn't bite me. I didn't use the yellow gloves, because I thought that might look weird.

"Can I touch it?" Duke asked.

"After the picture," I said.

I held Bianca up to my cheek and she licked me. "So gross. I have lizard spit on my face."

"So cool," Pierre said.

Right as Lola snapped the picture, the lizard clamped her mouth shut on my nose.

"Ack!" I said.

"The lizard facebombed you," Duke said, laughing.

"That's actually a funny subject line," I said. "Noll appreciates my sense of humor."

So while I was surrounded by my middle school friends, I sent Noll Beck a picture of me and his lizard.

I hope you're feeling better. FYI your lizard facebombed me!

And Noll Beck wrote back right away. He said:

I'm getting there. Thanks for the update!

"Ooh. He gave me an exclamation point. And he just sent me a picture," I said.

I clicked to enlarge it and saw something very sad:

Noll Beck in what looked like a hospital bed, wearing what looked like a sling, next to what looked like his ex-girlfriend.

"Cute nurse," Pierre said.

But Sylvie understood that we were not looking at Noll's nurse.

"Life is long," Sylvie said. "That picture doesn't mean anything."

But it meant something to me. Because Noll Beck's ex-girlfriend was hugging him.

"Let's start the DVD," Lola said. "Follow me."

Lola led Pierre and Duke out to my living room. I kept looking at the picture. I wasn't crushed. Just surprised. And a little bit sad.

"You're still the mascot. And people at your school think you're awesome. They can't wait to watch you cheer at the next game," Sylvie said. "You did it. You wanted to be popular and now you are."

I nodded. Then I closed the picture.

"Are you sad?" Sylvie asked.

"Not really," I said. "I have a pretty good life. Great friends. Grandma is back. According to Vicki Docker I possess a very powerful inner cheer beast."

"You're forgetting the most important thing," Sylvie said.

"I'm getting good grades in all my classes?" I asked.

"No."

"I'm not grounded?"

"No."

"My birthday is coming up?"

"No."

"What?" I asked. I was tired of guessing.

"You're awesome!" Sylvie yelled.

I didn't think Sylvie had ever told me that I was awesome before. It made me smile.

"Come watch the movie and be awesome in the living room!" Lola called.

I walked down the hallway, feeling better and better with each step. Maybe middle school was going to be a lot more fun than I'd thought. Now that I'd defeated T.J. and become popular, maybe things were going to be amazing for me. Maybe Grandma had been right all along.

Happiness isn't something you chase. It's just the way you feel.

KRISTEN TRACY grew up in a small town in Idaho, where she learned a lot about bears. She now lives in San Francisco, where she volunteers as a gardener on Alcatraz. She has written many books for teens and tweens and people younger than that, including *Lost It, Crimes of the Sarahs, A Field Guide for Heartbreakers, Sharks & Boys, Camille McPhee Fell Under the Bus,* and *The Reinvention of Bessica Lefter.*